Seeking THE STAR

—◆— A CHILTON CROSSE NOVEL —◆—

TRACI BORUM

Unlocking New Worlds

Seeking The Star

Copyright © 2014 by Traci Borum. All rights reserved.

First Print Edition: July 2015

ISBN-13: 978-1-940215-54-9
ISBN-10: 1940215544

Red Adept Publishing, LLC
104 Bugenfield Court
Garner, NC 27529
http://RedAdeptPublishing.com/

Cover and Formatting: Streetlight Graphics

Dedicated to my beloved grandparents.
I'm honored to have you in my life, and I'm blessed
to be part of your strong spiritual legacy.
I love you.

Chapter One

The desolation of a winter night sat brooding on the earth, and in the sky. But, the red light came cheerily towards him from the windows.

~ Charles Dickens

NO ONE IN THE VILLAGE saw the dark shadow stagger forward, his feet stamping deep craters in powdery snow. No one heard the thump of his weary heart or saw the tremble of his fingers clutching the silver angel.

He trudged forward, relieved that the night covered him so well. The late hour meant villagers were tucked warmly in their beds, oblivious to him. He could pass through the town, undetected, hours before they awoke. He craved darkness—everywhere, at all times—so he could travel in solitude, never speaking to another soul. He knew, someday, he would have to face the light and be held accountable. Things had a way of being discovered. But at least for the moment, he could remain invisible.

He blinked snowflakes from his eyelashes and realized he didn't even know which Cotswold village he was traveling through. They all looked the same—a main street flanked with pristine limestone buildings, always dotted with quaint shops, a pub, a grocer's, and a novelty shop. And always tucked away at the edge were a church with a vicarage, several scattered cottages, and perhaps a farmhouse or two.

Like all the other villages, so late at night, it should have been dark, save for a streetlamp or maybe the soft glow of light beaming from deep within one of the shops. But the stranger saw cheery Christmas lights winking up ahead. At the end of the main road stood a Tudor cottage draped generously with multicolored lights. Everywhere. On hedges. On the rooftop. Even inside the front windows.

Someone certainly liked Christmas—more than liked it. From the look of things, the cottage's owners were fanatical. "We love Christmas!" the cottage seemed to scream at the top of its quaint little lungs.

Hating the reminder of the season—a representation of love, peace, forgiveness, and every other emotion he felt numb to—the stranger pressed on. He shifted the heavy bag he'd slung on his back, turning his face from the cheery lights as he trudged closer to the cottage. He picked up his speed, hoping to pass it quickly.

He didn't know how much longer he could survive without food, warmth, or sleep. But he did know that he had to keep moving, because as long as his feet slogged forward, his mind could slog forward, too. The moment he brought it all to a halt, the past would catch up with him, and he would be doomed. He must carry on.

But without warning, his body betrayed him, and his legs gave out. He felt himself stumble and fall, with no energy or strength to stop it...

Mary Cartwright rubbed her tired eyes under her glasses and blinked twice to correct the dryness. After readjusting the pillow on her lap, she carried on with her needlepoint—her only cure for insomnia. She pierced the patterned fabric with her needle then pulled it back again with expert fingers. No need for a thimble.

Nearly sixty years ago, when she was a little girl, her grandmother had taught her how to needlepoint. Mary had lost count of the many pillows and wall hangings she'd made for people over those decades. So, on a late evening on the first of December, she was finishing a gift for a great-niece who lived in Essex.

Earlier, she'd tried in vain to settle in next to her husband and doze off. The silence had kept her awake. She blamed the snow, the first real snow of the season, which had started falling hours before. Odd, how something as light and feathery as snow created a heavy hush that seemed oppressive, able to penetrate the thick walls of Mistletoe Cottage and render her restless. She had given up on sleep and gently drawn back the covers, so as not to awaken her snoring husband. Bootsie, their nine-year-old cat, had insomnia, too. He'd followed her into the sitting room and snuggled up by the fire, which she'd stoked into a comforting blaze. He closed his eyes and licked his fur in long, meticulous strokes.

Though Mary had been rocking by the fireside since then, needlepointing, she couldn't get warm enough. The inescapable cold had seeped into every crevice of the cottage. Frustrated, she reached for the heavy quilt folded on the arm of the sofa, planning to cover her icy ankles.

But when she extended her hand, she heard something—a muffled *thud* outside her front door, like someone falling, like a male someone large enough to create a *thud*. Mary gasped, frozen in place.

She forced herself to move, setting her needlepoint silently on the ottoman. Her eyes remained on the front door, unblinking. Perhaps the late hour and solitude had pricked her thoughts, creating anxiety, but the longer she stood staring, the more she envisioned that person charging through it at any moment, guns blazing. Bootsie had already scampered back into the bedroom for refuge, leaving Mary to fend for herself.

Why did George have to be such a heavy sleeper? She would have to go it alone, face her irrational fears, and glance outside. Surely there was no danger involved. It would be fine. Only a peek…

She approached the front window, which blinked with festive lights, and tipped back the thick linen curtain gingerly.

Immediately, she saw the dark outline—the body of a man, crumpled in the snow, facedown. Snowflakes had begun to collect on his back as he lay unmoving. She strained to see his face, but it was turned away from her.

Time to awaken George. This man was no attacker. He needed their help. She most surely could not handle the situation alone.

She padded down the narrow hallway with quiet urgency and attempted to rouse her husband. She tried everything—jostling his shoulder, flooding the room with light, even whisper-yelling directly into his ear. He only flinched, gulped, then rolled over to continue his snoring.

It was extreme, but Mary knew what would work. With all her strength and all her might, she nudged at George's back, pushing him carefully toward the opposite edge of the bed—farther, farther, until he began to topple over it. She knew the distance would be short—their thirty-year-old bed sat extremely low to the ground. He hit the floor and produced the second muffled thud she'd heard that evening.

"What in blazes...?" His balding head appeared from the other side of the bed as he gathered himself and stared at his wife with a groggy frown. "Are you trying to kill me?"

"Hardly, George. Don't be ridiculous. You wouldn't wake up," she whispered accusingly. "Are you all right? Anything broken?"

"I can't tell yet. Let me get up."

"I need you to pay attention. We have a crisis."

"What is it?" His eyes wide, he stood and rubbed the small of his back with a groan.

"There's a man. Outside. I think he's been hurt."

"A man?"

"I heard something. I was needlepointing, and then there was a thud. We don't have time for all this." She waved at him to follow. "Come and help me."

He obeyed, stepping into his shoes along the way, and by the time they finally reached the front door, she hoped the stranger hadn't disappeared. She hated to think she might have nearly killed her husband for no reason at all.

Rather than crack the door and peek through, Mary decided to fling it open. "See?" she proclaimed, letting in a blast of frigid air and drifts of snow. She reached for her long coat on the rack and found her shoes. The moment George saw the man lying motionless, two meters outside the cottage's small front garden, he sprang into action, as though he'd gulped down three cups of strong coffee—no matter that he wore only his striped pajamas with no coat. His nimble instincts were due to his training as a medic in the war. Mary had seen him respond that way before—he knew precisely what to do. George was a confident man who took charge when it mattered. Those qualities had drawn her to him when they'd first met.

He dropped to the stranger's side to check his vitals. Mary saw the side of the man's face—well, as much as she *could* see through the scraggly dark beard clotted with snow. Longish dark hair peeked out the sides of the knit cap he wore—a "skull" cap, she remembered the young people calling them. The man appeared to be in his mid-forties, but he

4

might have looked even younger without the beard. He let out a quiet moan and winced, his eyes still closed. Fortunately, the falling snow had lessened to a few occasional flakes.

"Can you hear me, son?" George asked.

"Amanda," the stranger mumbled then slipped back into oblivion.

"What will we do?" Mary asked as a rush of ice-cold air nipped at her cheeks and her ankles.

"Let's see if we can get him inside."

"Our cottage?"

"Yes, love. There's no other way. We can't leave him out here."

"Of course not. No."

George grasped the man under the shoulders in an attempt to hoist him up, but George wasn't strong enough. The stranger was at least six feet tall, and George was a mere five feet six.

"I can't do it," he whispered, out of breath.

The stranger groaned, then his eyes fluttered open and focused on George's face.

"Son, can you hear me?" George tried again. "Do you think you can raise yourself up? You can lean on me."

The man nodded then rose and took a couple of significant stumbles. The impression of his body remained in the snow, like a chalk outline at a crime scene. Mary noticed something wedged beside the outline—something shiny reflecting the blinking lights nearby. Mary stooped to pluck up the object then dusted off the snow. A silver angel, a pendant of some sort, glittered in her hand. *Beautiful.*

"Mary, love, get his bag, please?" George grunted, helping maneuver the man's arm around his shoulders.

Mary reached down for the bag and found the weight impossible to lift on her own, especially with her bad back. So, she got creative and dragged it inside, along with an accumulated pile of snow.

Shutting the door, she abandoned the bag and watched George tip the shivering man into a sitting position on their sofa beside the fire. Then George removed the man's damp leather jacket, shoes, and socks. After that, he leaned the man backward to recline and covered him with the heavy quilt Mary had reached for minutes earlier. She could see the stranger's teeth chattering from across the room.

"I'll ring Dr. Andrews," George whispered, squeezing Mary's arm as he passed her to find his mobile phone. At the kitchen table, he tapped out the doctor's number. One ring, two rings, more rings. No response.

"I'll have to go and fetch him," George said, reaching for his coat on the rack.

"In the middle of the night?"

"It's only a precaution. This lad may have a serious injury. At the least, it appears he hit his head. We found him. Now we're responsible for him. It's the right thing to do."

"Yes, of course. You're right. But—"

"What?" he asked, buttoning up.

"You're going to leave me... alone? With him?" She pointed. "He's a perfect stranger."

George grinned through his beard. "You'll be fine. He's in no shape to do anything. Besides, I think he's passed out again." He pointed to the man, whose eyes were closed tightly. "I'll only be a moment. And I'll carry my mobile with me, in case you need to reach me." He shoved the phone into his pocket.

"All right," she agreed, feeling mildly better.

"Besides, you've got Bootsie to keep you company."

"Tsk. Hardly the same. He's still hiding in the bedroom!"

George gave his wife a wink and a kiss. Then he walked out the door, back into the snow.

In the silence, Mary could tell that her heart rate had elevated from all the excitement. Keeping an eye on the man, she inched over to the adjoining kitchen and found her pillbox on the counter beside the toaster. She snapped open the box's compartment, poured a glass of water, then swallowed her blood pressure pill with a generous sip.

During the entire fifteen minutes George left Mary alone, the stranger moved only once, repositioning himself with a mumble. By the time George returned with a disheveled Dr. Andrews, Mary had relaxed. The man was harmless, indeed. And by the scruffy look of him, he was more vagabond than thief or murderer.

Mary stood back while Dr. Andrews crouched at the stranger's side, checked his vitals and temperature, and examined his eyes with a penlight. Then he spoke to the man, who opened his eyes, whispered a few words, then closed his eyes again.

Dr. Andrews rose with a grunt, his seventy-year-old knees giving him trouble, and turned to George and Mary. "Probable dehydration and hypothermia. No sign of concussion that I can see. Still, the lad's in poor shape."

Mary's gaze returned to the man on her sofa, and an inexplicable sympathy filled her heart. He had been dropped at their doorstep for a reason. He might've died out there in the snow, if not for Mary's insomnia.

"What does he need?" Mary asked Dr. Andrews. "How can we help him recuperate?"

"Keep him warm. Liquids tonight, then soft foods when he's ready. And rest. Lots of rest. That's what he needs the most, at this point. If his condition worsens—vomiting or dizziness, especially—don't hesitate to ring me."

"Thank you, Jim." George shook his hand. "I appreciate your coming out here so late."

"Yes," Mary chimed in. "Let me put the kettle on before you go."

"No, no." Dr. Andrews waved in protest. "I must get back. Early schedule tomorrow. Thank you for the offer, though."

George escorted the doctor out, thanking him again, then locked the door. "Well, this was certainly an unexpected twist in our evening."

"Yes, indeed. He needs some hot tea. Or water," she insisted.

"He's asleep. Let's leave him be. We can nourish him in the morning. He can drink all the tea you want him to drink then."

"But you heard what the doctor said. Dehydration—"

"You're welcome to try, Mary, but look at him. Sound asleep. Probably needs rest more than he needs fluids. He'll be fine for a few hours."

"Do you think he's warm enough?" She watched the man's chest rise and fall with deep, purposeful breaths. "Perhaps another blanket?"

"We don't want him too warm," George said. "He's close to the fire and looks quite bundled up. No more chattering teeth, see?"

"True," she said, semi-satisfied.

"Come to bed, Mary. He'll be fine." George reached out to nudge her in the right direction. "He's indoors, out of the cold, the doctor's seen to him. All is well."

She agreed reluctantly, knowing she wouldn't be able to sleep a single wink. "Oh! I forgot something. You go on. I'll be there in a minute." She patted his arm and watched him shrug and yawn. He pivoted to go down the hall, scratching at his thick gray beard. He would surely be snoring before she joined him again.

Mary walked to the kitchen counter, where she'd set it down earlier, in order to swallow her pill. There it sat—the silver angel. Grasping it, she tiptoed over to where the sleeping man lay. When she placed the angel into his half-open palm, his fingers closed over it tightly, as though the angel belonged there and always had.

Mary tried to sleep. She wrestled with the covers, flipped her pillow, and even attempted an old trick of thinking the alphabet backward. But the image of the man, cold and malnourished, wouldn't leave her troubled mind.

So, an hour after she'd followed George to bed, she carefully peeled back the sheets, found her slippers in the dark with her toes, pulled on her dressing gown, then trudged down the hallway. The fire had dimmed, so she coaxed it back to life with the poker then switched her attention to the sofa. The man was sleeping, but his body twitched as his eyes roamed back and forth beneath his lids. He was wrestling with something. And the shivering had returned.

She took the quilt, which had fallen below his elbows, and tucked it back up beneath his chin. His fingers grasped the edges as he let out a long sigh.

Mary made her way to the kitchen and warmed a pot of broth on the Aga's stove top. Back in the sitting room again, she sat at the edge of the coffee table and waited patiently with the bowl of broth. When it was cool enough, she ladled the broth and held it close to his lips. His eyes remained closed, but his mouth reacted, sipping on autopilot. She dabbed the broth from his beard with a napkin she'd brought from the kitchen.

She spent the next half hour that way, one spoonful at a time, until he'd consumed half the bowl. Finally, she could sleep.

Chapter Two

But I am sure I have always thought of Christmas time... as a good time; a kind, forgiving, charitable, pleasant time.

~ Charles Dickens

MARY HALF-EXPECTED TO AWAKEN AND see an empty sofa. She thought perhaps the stranger had been a figment of her wild imagination, or had regained consciousness in the early-morning hours and decided to disappear.

But when she rounded the corner of the sitting room, there he lay, in almost the same position she'd left him. The fire had sputtered down to ashes, and his blanket had been kicked off. He was shivering again.

"Oh! Poor dear." She hastily tied the belt of her dressing gown and approached carefully, trying not to startle him awake. She'd managed to pull the quilt up over him, almost to his neck, before she heard a voice.

"How's our patient?" George asked her from behind.

"Shh!" She turned around. "Still sleeping."

George smiled, lovingly patronizing her. "Well, he needs to wake up *some*time. He'll need to eat, get his strength back."

"What time is it?" she asked with a gasp.

George, dressed and ready for work, was clear evidence that she had overslept. She always arose before he did, laid out his socks, made him a hot breakfast, and kissed him good-bye. "You didn't wake me!"

"You needed your rest. You had a long night."

"But your breakfast..."

"I'll pick up something at the bakery on my way."

Her eyes narrowed. "George, really. A scone? You know that's not good for your waistline. Or your heart."

"I'll choose wisely. No scones."

"Promise?"

"I promise."

She plucked a stray piece of lint from his shoulder and brushed the fabric with her fingertips. His white shirt and gray trousers were pressed and sharp, just as she'd prepared them yesterday. She never wanted him to leave the cottage looking rumpled. *Old* men looked rumpled and out of use. She never wanted people to see George that way—because that wasn't how she saw him.

"You get to work, now." She coaxed him toward the door. "You'll be late. Especially with that extra stop at the bakery."

"Yes, dear." He kissed her cheek, and his whiskers scratched her skin as they always did. "By the way," he added as he reached for his coat, "I think we should keep this... situation... to ourselves. For a bit. You know how the gossips would love to hear about the stranger who was rescued in the middle of the night. It could turn into quite a scandal. Lots of questions. I think our boy needs a bit of privacy while he recuperates."

"Agreed. Now, off you go! You're practically Father Christmas this month, with all those deliveries you'll be making!"

He put on his cap and tipped it. "We aim to please."

She watched him leave, still proud of him after all these years. Hard worker that he was, George Cartwright had been the primary postman for the village for the past thirty-five years. In his late twenties, after a decade in the Royal Navy, he had wanted a simple country life. So he'd put his finger on a map and selected the tiny Cotswold village of Chilton Crosse. He became a junior assistant at the post office, helping to sort the post and relieve the desk clerk during her breaks. That was how Mary had met him, in fact, while running an errand for her father, to purchase stamps. She'd walked into the post office to see a new employee—handsome, ambitious, jovial. She was smitten at first sight.

Even past retirement age, George still wanted to work. He had a youthful spirit, was stocky and strong, and had plenty of strength and energy left in him. Besides, to give up the post office would be to give up part of his social life, in a sense. He'd made a career out of having friendly conversations with the villagers. He'd become a brief but important part of their daily lives, enquiring about one person's illness or another person's new grandchild. He knew practically every tidbit about everyone in the village. Still, Mary had learned long ago not to weasel things out of him. The villagers told him so much private information because they trusted him. Perhaps when he finally did retire, she could wheedle a few juicy secrets from him...

Out of the corner of her eye, Mary saw the stranger stir. He scratched his beard and squinted at the bright sunlight streaming in through the front window.

Mary hurried to fill a glass of water for him. Then she returned to his side and offered it shyly, feeling her nerves return. She had no idea what to expect.

He inched up, muscle by muscle, to a sitting position.

"How do you feel?" she asked. "The doctor said you have hypothermia. And dehydration. I brought you some water—"

"Doctor?" he asked, making eye contact for the first time. "Where am I?" His voice held the rasp of one that hadn't been used for days. His accent sounded a bit posh, like a Londoner's. It surely didn't fit the tatty man on her sofa.

"You're safe," she assured him. "You're in Chilton Crosse. A Cotswold village. We—my husband and I—found you, out in the snow last night. You had collapsed."

His sapphire-blue eyes were stern at first but then softened. The bags under them told her he hadn't slept in days and days. She handed him the glass of water, and he took it. The first sip was a challenge, as he sputtered and gagged. But then he seemed to get his sea legs back and swallowed several quick sips in a row.

"Are you warm enough?" she asked.

He took the last gulp then nodded and handed back the glass. His trembling hands told her he was lying.

"I'm going to prepare you some hot soup." She set down the glass and stooped over to add another log to the fire.

"Where's the, err..." He pointed his finger around the room. "The loo?"

"Oh. Yes, of course. Down the hall, to your right." She watched him sway, struggling to stand. Her instinct was to move forward and help, offer an arm, but something told her he wanted to do it on his own.

11

"Take your time," she said cheerily as she stoked the fire. Then she headed for the kitchen.

Thankfully, she'd made a hearty batch of chicken noodle soup two days ago, when George had started showing signs of a mild cold. She warmed it on the stove top, stirring now and then, and wondered what the day might bring. Her plans had changed instantly with the arrival of the stranger. Not that her plans had been all that glamorous to begin with—purchase some lace to send to her sister in Bath, start addressing her Christmas cards, and finish the wash. Nothing that couldn't wait. Although she would have to decide what to tell Holly about the next day's shift. Mary was only a volunteer at the Book Shoppe, but during the busy Christmas season, her absence might be felt in a pinch...

Breaking her thoughts, the man entered the sitting room and headed to the adjoining kitchen. Bootsie followed, sniffing at his bare feet. As the man sat at the breakfast table, he resembled a ninety-year-old, moving at a snail's pace, stiff and aching.

Mary busied herself with her task. She poured steaming soup into an ample bowl, filled a cup with strong tea, broke off a handful of crusty bread, and organized it all onto a dinner tray. She lifted it, careful not to strain the chronic arthritis in her wrist, and walked toward the table. When Mary placed it in front of him, he stared at the food with vacant eyes, picked up the spoon, and inhaled the steam from the pool of broth.

"It might take a few bites before your stomach adjusts," Mary reassured. "But it'll be good for you. I promise."

He took a cautious first sip, wincing as the broth went down. He took another sip, then another, and before long, he'd emptied half the bowl. Mary tried not to stare as he ate, but she couldn't help noticing the chunk of gold on his wrist—what appeared to be an extremely valuable watch, one of those Rolex pieces, maybe. Something else about him that didn't quite... fit.

"May I ask," she said softly, "what is your name?"

He swallowed and paused, as though debating whether a name would be too personal to give out. Then he said, "Ben," and dipped his spoon back into what was left of the soup.

"I'm Mary. Mary Cartwright. And my husband is George."

He nodded and shifted his attention to the tea.

Realizing that was all she would get out of him this morning, Mary went to pour herself a cup of tea. Though she craved more detail, she refused to be the overbearing, nosy type—no matter how much she wanted to be. In his own good time, he would reveal more. *Baby steps,* she told herself.

Behind her, she heard a quiet, "Thank you, Mrs. Cartwright."

She smiled and watched the dark golden nectar swirl around inside the cup.

She shouldn't have felt guilty, but she did. Rummaging through someone else's property might have bordered on being illegal.

Mary shoved aside the guilt and continued digging through Ben's bag. He couldn't very well continue to dress in filthy clothes for the next couple of days. She was a firm believer that clean clothes made a person feel instantly better. Something about the fresh scent offered a fresh outlook.

Earlier, after the soup, Ben had returned to the sofa, bundled up beneath the quilt, and fallen fast asleep again. Once she was certain he would be out for a while, Mary approached his bag, which was still sitting on the floor after the chaos of the previous night. She'd dragged it into the spare bedroom and sat on her knees to sort through it. Her only intention was to retrieve his dirty clothes and give them all a proper wash-up. Though tempted to peek through the bag's many side pockets, which likely held clues to his life, she paused and decided against it. *No.* She would not take advantage of the stranger. Her job here was to help, not to pry.

So, she abandoned the smaller side compartments and unzipped the largest part of the bag. Within minutes, she'd found—amongst a toothbrush case, shaving kit, and nearly empty box of Pepcid—four wrinkled and smelly T-shirts, three pairs of jeans, two expensive-feeling sweaters, and several pairs of socks and underwear. She could launder them before he even woke up. She hoped he wouldn't be livid with her for going through his bag. She didn't know him well enough to anticipate his reaction. Still, she would take her chances.

The mundane act of folding laundry shouldn't have been emotional. *They're only clothes,* Mary told herself. *Just common, everyday fabrics.*

But as she laid out the enormous chocolate-brown sweater on the breakfast table and folded neat creases, something familiar settled in the center of her stomach. The last time she'd laundered a tall young man's clothes, her son had been twenty years old. In fact, he'd been very close to Ben's height.

It had always struck her as comical, her son's height. She and George were considered petite people—well, *short,* really—their parents and grandparents had all been short, as well. How, then, had Mary and George been blessed with such a tall son? One who towered over everyone and even played basketball at university? One who had to hunch in order to hug his mother or duck in order to pass beneath the cottage's low door headers?

The chocolate sweater turned wavy, and Mary realized she was crying.

"Oh, dear," she whispered, abandoning the sweater and reaching for a tissue. She couldn't let her emotions get the best of her and distract her from the task at hand. Besides, Ben had nothing whatsoever to do with Mary's son. By all appearances, this man was a wanderer, a drifter who would probably leave them as suddenly as he'd fallen at their doorstep. She must push aside her own selfish memories and cater to this stranger in need.

She heard the doorknob turn and started shushing George before he even crossed the threshold.

"He's still sleeping," she warned.

"*Still?*"

"Yes. But he did get up for soup a few hours ago."

"Well. That's something." He removed his coat then paused before kissing his wife. "You all right? Your cheeks look red."

Mary remembered her tears and gave a casual, reassuring wave. "I'm a little flushed from doing some chores, dusting, whatnot. Why are you home early?"

"Had some unexpected help from the Murdoch boys. They needed extra spending money, and we had plenty for them to do."

"How nice."

Mary returned to her laundry, peeking over at Ben, whose chest rose and fell with deep breaths. His eyebrows were no longer crinkled into that permanent frown he wore, even in his sleep. For the first time since she'd laid eyes on him, he seemed peaceful.

"Can you watch him for about an hour?" she asked George.

"Watch him?" he whispered back. "You make him sound like a child we're babysitting. Or a dog."

She play-thumped his arm with her free hand. "That's not what I meant. It's just... he still seems a little disoriented. I'd hate for him to wake up with no one here. I've got a couple of errands to run, and I want to return before dark. The sun sets so quickly during these winter days..."

"Go on. I'm only messing about. Take as long as you need."

She folded the last T-shirt swiftly, with expert fingers, and added it to the finished stack. "These are his," she instructed. "They're all cleaned and pressed." She took her long wool coat from the rack and handed it to George. "There's more soup in the refrigerator if he should wake up. You can heat it on the stove top."

George held the coat as Mary threaded her arms through.

"Don't worry about us. We'll be fine," he reassured her. "Go on, and take your time."

"Thank you, dear." She pulled her gloves from the pockets and found her handbag nearby as George opened the door.

Immediately, the brisk air chilled her lungs and froze her cheeks. But she loved it. A few measly flakes drifted from a gray sky, but they were enough to make her smile. Mary thought about how rapidly Christmas would come and go. It was only the second of December, but the final month had a tendency to fly by faster than any other month did. So she wanted to savor every snowflake, every twinkling light, every gold ribbon, and every garland strand.

Gazing at the village, she sensed a rush of childlike excitement. Her home, Mistletoe Cottage, stood at the outskirts of Storey Road, the village's main street, and several meters away from George's post office, the first structure in a row of pristine limestone shops. She could see the entire street, in fact, from her doorstep. The village came alive in

December, partly for the tourists and partly for the residents. Every shop had worked tirelessly the past week, hanging festive decorations. They had coordinated their efforts, each shop using white lights of the same size to give a unified effect. They also displayed Christmas merchandise inside front windows—all mixed with golds, greens, and reds. Strung overhead between the shops, in perfect alignment, hung enormous evergreen wreaths. Soon, Mr. Elton would make his horses available for sleigh rides, and of course, then there was the Dickens Festival during the final week of December.

So much to look forward to...

Holly Newbury's bookshop stood at the other end of the street, six shops down. The distance was a nice little walk, during which Mary could stop and chat or wave at someone across the way. As tempted as she was to visit the bakery for gingerbread and mulled cider, she didn't have time.

Turning the brass knob in her gloved hand, she entered the Book Shoppe to that familiar scent—strong coffee, new books, and at this time of year, peppermint.

"Mrs. Cartwright! I didn't think I'd see you until tomorrow," Holly said, approaching her. "Do you fancy a coffee? Or tea?"

"No, dear. Thank you. I only have a moment. I wanted to let you know I won't be in tomorrow. I hope that doesn't produce any problems."

"No, of course not." She offered a beautiful, youthful smile.

Holly had plenty of reason to smile. She'd opened a thriving bookshop a few months ago, moved into a wee cottage of her own on her family's property, and fallen madly in love with a young man. Early last summer, Holly had met Fletcher Hays, an American from Texas, and the whole village had buzzed about their friendship. Holly had denied their connection early on, but Mrs. Cartwright had seen instantly, at the weekly book club, the way Fletcher's gaze lingered on Holly when she wasn't looking. *Meant to be*, Mary remembered thinking when Holly had finally come to her senses.

"I hope nothing's wrong," Holly said through a frown of concern.

"Oh, no. Everything's fine. I have some... unexpected business to take care of. I hope that's all right."

"Mrs. Cartwright, you won't even let me pay you. It's *more* than all right. I appreciate any time you're willing to give. You're a treasure."

"Well, thank you." Mary felt her cheeks flush.

Her volunteer days had begun two months ago, when she'd noticed a few bored, rowdy children wrestling in the nook at the corner of the shop.

Realizing the parents had no intention of stepping in, Mary walked into the nook and past the children then assessed their average age. She chose a book from the shelf—an old favorite of hers, Beatrix Potter's *Peter Rabbit*. She sat on the stool, opened the book, and began to read aloud. The children soon released their holds on each other and sat, too. They folded their legs and arms and stared, mesmerized as Mary showed them the colorful pictures.

Holly saw what was happening, and afterward, she'd asked if Mrs. Cartwright would consider holding a regular, weekly story hour. The answer was an instant yes, under the condition that Mary wouldn't accept any money. She didn't want monetary value attached to something that didn't feel like work. Since then, she'd entered the shop early on some days, helped out when the children were in school, filled the gaps for Holly by shelving books, made coffee, and chatted with customers. It had provided a welcome outing each week that helped Mary stay productive and involved in the village.

"Oh. There was something I wanted to purchase while I'm here." Mary scanned the shelves. "Do you have a book that a young man might enjoy? Well, young to me. In his late thirties or thereabouts. It's... a sort of Christmas present," she clarified.

"I've got exactly the thing." Holly clicked her fingers together.

Mary followed her to the suspense section and watched Holly run her fingers along the novels' spines until she found the right one. "Here. *The Trident Deception*, by Rick Campbell, an American author. Sure to please any male, young or old. They're calling this author the next Tom Clancy. And Fletcher loved it, if that's any endorsement."

"Perfect. I'll take it." Mary thumbed through her pound notes to pay for the book.

"It's on me," Holly insisted, shaking her head. "I want to do this."

"Oh, no. I couldn't—"

"You can, and you will," Holly said, her tone firm but sweet.

"Well, if you're absolutely sure..."

"I am. Absolutely. Happy Christmas." Holly carried the book to the nearest counter, slid it inside a crisp, brown paper bag, and handed it over to Mary.

"Speaking of Fletcher, how is your young man?"

"He's wonderful. Thanks for asking. He starts his new teaching job at the school right after the holiday. He's thrilled."

"How lovely! He'll make a wonderful teacher. And how is... Frank?"

Holly shook her head. "Not well. He had to go on holiday. Get away for a while." Her voice dropped to a whisper. "I think it'll do him good. Noelle and I encouraged him to go to Cornwall and breathe in the fresh sea air. He's at her family cottage now, in fact."

Frank O'Neill, the art gallery's curator—and Holly's former boss—had recently suffered a heartbreak. His fiancée, Lily, had broken up with him suddenly. She was involved with another man, whom she'd met on the Internet. She'd left Frank's ring sitting on the gallery table three weeks ago, with only a brief note.

"He'll recover," Holly added. "I'm sure of it. It'll just take time."

"The poor dear..."

Mary noticed two customers lining up, clearing throats, ready to ask Holly questions. So Mary said a hasty good-bye and walked back out into the bleak midwinter, the book tucked securely under her arm. *Mission One accomplished. On to Mission Two.*

On the way to her final stop, Mary noticed the sky's light had faded significantly. She approached Mrs. Pickering's market, which was directly across the street, and paused to chuckle at two young boys in the road, pelting each other with snowballs. The snow certainly brought out the mischief in some.

"Good evening!" Mrs. Pickering called when Mary stepped inside.

"Hello, Mrs. Pickering." Mary knew, as always, that she couldn't get away with grabbing her selected items, paying, and leaving. A visit to Mrs. Pickering's was never that easy. Just as one was required to pay for one's items, one was also required to receive a heaping dose of Mrs. Pickering's village gossip or to endure an uncomfortable barrage of nosy questions. Neither was enjoyable, but Mary had learned long ago to nod amiably and listen quietly. The faster to get on her merry way.

Fortunately, another customer came to the counter, giving Mary the opportunity to grab a nearby basket and dart toward the first aisle. She'd already made her mental list on the walk over, and she found all the needed items in a few minutes.

She placed them on the counter, one by one, as Mrs. Pickering started in: "Did you hear about last night's little event?" She punched certain words for dramatic effect, raising her eyebrows along with them.

Genuinely curious, Mary made eye contact. "Event? No. What happened?"

"Well." She placed her elbows on the counter and leaned in to whisper, "Apparently, Dr. Andrews was called out in the middle of the night. Rather urgently."

"Oh?" Mary knew exactly where the story was going and diverted her eyes toward the counter. She had never been a good liar, and her heart raced at the thought of having to offer a false reaction—or worse, to come up with an untruth.

"Yes. I don't know many details. Only that some… tramp… collapsed in the street, and someone found him, nearly dead! Dr. Andrews even had to perform CPR!"

"Who was he?" Mary asked as casually as she could, fishing out the frozen peas from her basket, still unable to look Mrs. Pickering in the eye. "This… person?"

"It's a mystery," she replied. "He must still be in the village somewhere, recuperating. If he's not *dead*, that is."

"Hmm. Interesting."

"Isn't it?" Finally, Mrs. Pickering began tapping keys on the till, completing the order.

Eager for a change of subject, Mary brought up the forecasted mini-blizzard—eight inches of snow were predicted!—which gave her the four minutes of conversation she needed before finally leaving the market. Sometimes Mary wasn't certain Mrs. Pickering's items were worth the price of the awkward conversation. Especially today.

Returning home, her back aching and arms quivering under the weight of the groceries she carried, Mary struggled to reach the knob of Mistletoe Cottage with her fingers, so she knocked with her foot instead. A few seconds later, the door opened.

"Here," George said, seeing her loaded down. He took all four bags, including Holly's submarine novel clutched under Mary's arm, and marched the bags to the kitchen table.

The blazing fire George had recently made was too irresistible. Mary removed her gloves and walked straight toward it, stretching out her aching fingers. The immediate heat stung her cheeks, thawing them. She closed her eyes and sighed. *A lovely fire to banish away the cold like a warm embrace.*

Suddenly remembering their guest, she glanced to her left and saw the empty sofa, the quilt crumpled at one end, discarded.

"Where's Ben?" she asked George, who was busy unpacking the groceries.

"Who?"

"Our young man, of course! He didn't leave, did he?" She wriggled out of her coat and walked toward the kitchen, trying not to show her alarm.

"I put him in Sheldon's room. He woke up about an hour ago, so I heated up some soup. He ate half of it then started for the sofa again, but I pointed him in the direction of the bedroom. Thought he'd be more comfortable there."

Mary approved. "I'd had the same thought last night."

"So it's Ben, eh? You managed to nudge something out of him?"

"Not much," she admitted, tucking her still-cold hands inside her skirt pockets. "Only a first name. He was hesitant about even that, so I left it alone." She lowered her voice and inched closer to her husband. "Did you see the *watch*?"

George nodded and raised his eyebrows. "I don't think the lad's been homeless for very long. He would've sold that watch by now, if he needed to. Must be another story there..."

"Story?"

"Well, I think there's more to him than the beard and the standoffishness. He's not your typical vagabond. Not one who makes a habit of it, anyway. I suspect he's running away from something."

"I wonder what it could be."

"We'll probably never know." George shrugged. "In any case, he's settled in for the night. Did you finish your errands?"

"I did. Though Mrs. Pickering made it a challenge."

"Doesn't she always?" He snickered. "That woman can get under the skin of the most patient of men. Don't know how Mr. Pickering used to put up with it."

"Oh, George." She patted his ample waist as she reached for her apron, planning to tell him all about her outing over a dinner of chicken and dumplings.

Hours later, near midnight, both of them still contentedly full, Mary and George sat near the fire as they did every evening. Mary continued her needlepoint, and George read his script until he dozed off, which was usually around page five.

Earlier, Mary had tuned the radio to the "All Christmas, All the Time" station, despite George's grumblings. He never complained beyond the grumbling, though. He understood how crucial the holidays were to Mary, especially since the accident. It was her bit of therapy or perhaps avoidance—even Mary wasn't sure. Either way, over-celebrating the holidays worked to soothe her, so George always indulged her. He put up the lights each year, always earlier than anyone else in the village, and helped her deliver presents to nearly everyone in the village each Christmas Eve.

Just as Bing began to croon about the holly and the ivy, Mary heard a door crack open in the hallway behind her. She arched her neck to see Ben, who dipped his head to avoid hitting it on the doorframe.

"Good evening," Mary said, offering a warm smile. "Or, I guess I should say, nearly morning…"

"How long have I been out?" he asked, his monotone voice creaky from so much sleep. His long hair was matted on one side, and Mary noticed he was wearing one of the plaid shirts she'd washed and folded for him.

Mary did the math in her head and replied, "About ten hours." She placed aside her needlepoint. "How are you feeling? The doctor said to watch for nausea, headaches, that sort of thing."

Ben paused and shook his head. "Headache's gone. No nausea. Only a bad bruise where I hit my knee. Nothing that won't heal."

"Are you hungry?"

"Ravenous, actually." His stomach growled to confirm it.

She rose from the rocking chair, stiff from the day's activities. "I can fix that, easy peasy. You have a seat."

Mary busied herself in the kitchen, glad that she'd saved a plate of leftover dumplings. She heard her husband attempting conversation with Ben, but their voices were low and hard to make out. The tones were even, matter-of-fact. She was dying to hear every word, but she would pry it out of George later.

As she set the warmed-up plate on the kitchen table, the men got up to join her.

George protested to something Ben had just said: "No, son. Don't feel you have to—"

"Have to what?" Mary asked.

Ben approached her, pulled out his chair, and explained. "I should leave. Tomorrow. I've imposed on you good people enough." He sat and unfolded the napkin.

"But you mustn't," she insisted. "You're not well enough. You still need your rest. Besides, wherever will you go?"

Ben shrugged with one shoulder. "Not sure yet. Haven't thought it through."

"Well, anyway," she continued, "a huge snowstorm is forecasted for tomorrow. Eight inches of snow. You can't put yourself back out in that weather. It wouldn't be wise."

"Mary does have a point," George added, coming to stand beside her. "It's sensible, staying here with us, at least one more night. Besides, you'll have a harder time saying no to my wife than you will facing that snowstorm. Once she gets something in her head, it's set there for good. No use squirming out of it."

Mary wasn't completely sure whether that was a compliment or an insult, but either way, he was right. She knew the lengths of her own stubbornness. She could be quite convincing when she put her mind to it.

Ben smoothed out the napkin and said, almost too softly, "In that case... all right. One more night. Thank you."

He lifted his fork and speared a dumpling as Mary lifted her eyes and beamed at George.

Chapter Three

External heat and cold had little influence... No warmth could warm, no wintry weather chill him.

~ Charles Dickens

BEN GRANGER NEEDED A MOMENT to remember exactly where he was. His muscles aching, he sat up carefully, still clutching the angel. The dent in the center of his palm, where the wing had pressed into it all night, was painful. He clicked on the table lamp to see his surroundings more clearly. The cream-colored walls, the stone floors, the rocking chair in the corner with a sewing table nearby, and a tall bookcase were all neatly kept.

The day before, Mr. Cartwright had insisted Ben take "our Sheldon's room" instead of remaining on the sofa. Blinking his eyes into focus and leaning on one elbow, Ben studied the picture on the nightstand beside Sheldon's bed. A towering young man with a beaming smile was handing Mrs. Cartwright something, a gift maybe. The young man stood at least a foot and a half above his mother. They seemed happy, in sync. Ben wondered where the young man was. *Grown and living in another town, with a family of his own? Children, perhaps?*

When Ben rolled over again to rest his weary body, he discovered that something else was suddenly much more important than sleep. He needed a bath. Desperately.

As much as soap and water had powers to transform, to clear away grime and grit and soil, they still couldn't change the inside of a man. Ben stepped out of the too-small tub and reached for the fluffy green towel. He clutched it to his dripping face and closed his eyes tightly, wishing he could disappear inside the towel's softness. The firm pressure, the extreme darkness of pressing something hard against his eyelids had a way of shutting everything else out. But the sensation didn't last.

He exhaled deeply then dried himself off. Squeezing out the excess drops from his hair, he realized how long it had grown. He wrapped the towel around his waist and rubbed the mirror with the palm of his hand. Ben couldn't remember the last time he'd faced a mirror. The thick beard caught him off guard more than the length of his hair did. He was unrecognizable, even to himself—especially to himself.

He recalled that Mrs. Cartwright had given him an electric razor, along with a basket of toiletries she'd put beside the basin. Staying with the Cartwrights was like staying in the best of hotels—he had anything he needed, whenever he needed it. He shouldn't get used to that, though, depending on other people. It nearly always ended with someone getting disappointed. Or devastated.

Razor in hand, Ben paused. Maybe it was best to leave the beard alone. It mirrored how he felt inside—scraggly and unkempt. Perhaps a compromise was in order. He could keep it but trim it. Removing at least a few of the wiry bits would make the beard manageable again. Noticing a pair of trimming scissors, he set down the razor. After a few minutes of trimming, he dusted the tiny hairs from the basin into the palm of his hand, trying to make the surface as clean as he'd first found it. The least he could do was be a decent guest.

Ben stepped into his jeans—he'd lost ten pounds, at least—then he slipped on the navy sweater, which Mrs. Cartwright had laundered. His first thought when he'd seen the neat stack of folded clothes had been: *What else did she see?* He thought of the zippered pockets in his bag and hoped they hadn't been *un*zipped. But her demeanor told him she probably hadn't peeked. It didn't matter anyway. The pockets' contents didn't give any secrets away or contain any revelations about the life he was running from. Just the thought of that other life caused the pain to return, like a sharp knife in the dead center of his abdomen. He placed his hand on the counter and bore down, waiting for the pain to subside. He recognized exactly what it was—the start of an ulcer. All the symptoms were there. For the moment, though, he would have to endure the pain. It was the least he deserved.

Feeling claustrophobic in the miniature loo built for miniature people, Ben opened the door to a snap of cold air, a stark contrast from the virtual steam room he'd been inside for the past forty-five minutes. He could hear one of the Cartwrights snoring from another room.

Antsy, Ben tiptoed into the sitting room, where a soft meow greeted him. A white cat with black paws lay atop the sofa like a statue, staring at him with green marble eyes. Ben scanned the room and saw Christmas tree lights blinking in the corner. He hadn't noticed a tree before—or the piano nearby it. No wonder, since Christmas decorations, primarily a snowy cotton landscape with miniature ice skaters and a pond, covered every part of it.

Christmas everywhere. He couldn't escape it.

He went through to the kitchen and noticed the new bottle of antacid tablets sitting conspicuously by itself in the dead center of the table. Mrs. Cartwright had probably seen the nearly empty one in his bag and found him a replacement.

After popping two tablets, he thought about what to do next. Rather than raid the kitchen for something to eat—which, he suspected, Mrs. Cartwright wouldn't have minded and would, in fact, have insisted upon—he preferred to go out and see where his stomach led him. Plus, feeling significantly more clearer-headed since his shower, he'd developed a sudden case of cabin fever. His lungs craved fresh air, snowstorm or no snowstorm.

He found a notepad beside the kitchen landline and scrawled a quick message to Mrs. Cartwright. Then he retrieved his jacket, which still contained his wallet in one pocket and his gloves and cap in the other, though he didn't recall tucking them there. He had no memory of the night he'd collapsed, except for trudging toward the cottage. Ben realized his good fortune—taken in by kind people who'd fed him hot soup by a roaring fire. He was safe, for the first time in a long time.

He put on his cap and gloves then quietly opened the door as the cat meowed at him again. The sky was a muted gray, and the packed snow that crunched under Ben's work boots told him no snow had fallen recently. He hunched into the stabbing wind, grateful for a change of scenery. The itch he'd felt to leave was so strong, he'd even thought of sneaking out that morning—of packing his bag, leaving behind a thank-you note, and going on to the next village, wherever that might have been. But he'd given his word. He couldn't bear the expression Mrs. Cartwright's face would hold as she read his good-bye note. So, a brief outing would have to tide him over.

The first shop he saw was an art gallery, which reminded him exactly of one he and Amanda had visited in Cornwall about three years back, on holiday. With the same limestone front and crisscross windows, it had the same quaint feel. Before he could make the decision to go inside, his hand had already reached for the knob. He didn't even know if the gallery was open, but he let the knob turn in his hand then walked inside.

The dimmed lights and quiet atmosphere soothed his senses. He saw paintings hung along the wall, each one lit by a circle of soft light, as if to beckon the visitor with a crooking finger. "Come inside. Come and see…"

He stepped to the first painting—a tranquil, colorful country scene of the Cotswolds in spring, with lush green hills, fluffy sheep, and the hint of a church steeple in the distance.

"A personal favorite of mine," a female said from behind. She was American; he could tell by her accent. Ben swiveled his neck and saw a petite, beautiful—and very pregnant—blonde standing with her arms crossed over her belly.

Ben reached for his cap and removed it.

"I'm sorry to startle you," she said with a friendly smile.

"No, you didn't."

"I love the perspective of it. This one." She pointed back to the canvas. "The hills look so close, you can almost touch them—but the steeple seems far away."

"Yes." Ben pointed, too, at the painting's corner. "And there's a hint of a sunset beyond that tree. An orange glow."

"Exactly. Such nice detail, if you know how to look for it. Well, I'll leave you to browse. I'm the gallery owner, Noelle Spencer. Please let me know if you have any questions." She disappeared, leaving Ben to himself.

Despite the woman's pleasant demeanor, Ben was thankful not to have to enter into any further conversation. The less he had to explain about his situation, the better. Personal questions were his enemy. People usually meant well, but he never knew how to answer without sounding dismissive or rude. He clutched at his privacy like a dog with a juicy bone he dared not share.

He decided to stay a while, in the quiet. He moved from painting to painting, noticing the techniques and the transitions of color. He hadn't been very observant of art before he'd met Amanda. She'd shown him the value in it, the intricate creativity of separate strokes blending together, and particularly, of art's connection to history and emotion.

He moved along, focused on the final canvas. Aside from a couple of darker-themed works, most of these paintings were innocent, idealistic views of the world—perfect summer days, smiling faces, and bright sanguine colors. His world used to be colored, too.

Feeling edgy, Ben turned his back on the paintings and replaced his cap as he walked to the front door, bracing for the unforgiving blast of cold. He had no idea where he was going or what his plan was. Outside, he noticed more shops were starting to open. Shopkeepers unlocked doors, flicked on lights, and waved at each other across the street.

Beyond a stone gazebo in the center of the road, Ben spotted a pub called Joe's. Pubs weren't usually open until noon, but some of the best breakfasts he'd ever had were in those few pubs that did open early. So, he crossed the street, dodging a teenager on a bicycle, and approached the pub door at the exact time as a silver-haired man. They did an awkward step-forward-and-hesitate dance, wondering who would enter first. Finally, the silver-haired man opened the door with a grin and held it for Ben.

"Cheers," he said, walking through.

"No trouble," the man replied in a distinctly Scottish accent.

At the center of the pub stood a great beast of a bar. The U-shaped glossy mahogany behemoth was decorated in tinsel and lights. Christmas had been invited into every corner of the pub—from miniature stockings hanging above the bar, to mischievous cardboard elves decorating each table.

A stocky man stood behind the bar, setting shot glasses in a neat row, steaming hot from a dishwasher. Seeing his customers walk in, he stopped to greet them, wiping his hands on a dishtowel. "Morning." He greeted Ben with a nod. "And a frigid one, at that, eh?"

He seemed a cheerful sort, probably well liked by people. The local pub often became the barometer by which an entire village could be measured. If the barman was any indication, Chilton Crosse was a particularly gregarious one.

The silver-haired man took a left at the bar, walking toward a back staircase. "Room two, aye?" he asked the barman.

"That's the one. Can't get the bugger to drain. Thanks, Mac!" he yelled as the Scotsman disappeared up the stairs. The barman turned back to Ben. "Now. How can I help you?"

Faced with such a jovial personality, Ben felt obligated to find a smile. Why burden someone else with his dour mood? His attempt was forced, but he tried anyway. "Are you open for breakfast?"

"Right, we are!" He pointed to a chalkboard behind him, which listed the specials.

Ben pulled up a leather-covered stool and sat as he studied the menu. Though his appetite urged him toward the greasy and filling bubble and squeak, his pending ulcer helped him decide on something safer—an omelet. "I'll have the Number Four."

"Mushrooms?"

"Please."

"It'll be right out."

The man disappeared, and Ben was once again grateful for an empty bar. Except for that Mac person, Ben was the only one there. To his right, a blazing fire caught his attention. It spat and popped, beckoning him. Obeying, he got up from the stool and took a seat at the table near the fire.

Not even five minutes after Ben stared into the flames, hypnotized by their dance, the barman appeared at his side and set down a plate and a glass. "Something besides water?" he asked.

"No. Water's fine," Ben said.

"Here's your bill. Pay whenever you're ready. I'll be at the bar."

Ben tried once again to produce the smile, but he couldn't summon it. He picked up his fork and tucked in. The omelet melted in his mouth. He didn't remember ever eating anything so delicious. Well, not in the past several weeks, at least.

In a matter of moments, he had polished his plate and fished out his money. As he took his last swallow of water, Ben saw Mac round the corner and talk to the barman. He couldn't hear the exact words, but the mannerisms and the facial expressions told Ben they were mates, probably good ones. Ben used to have mates like that—ones who knew what university he attended, what kind of car he drove, or even sat with him in the hospital while the beeping of his wife's monitors drove him slowly insane.

Pushing down his envy, knowing he might never be brave enough to let anyone close enough to be a mate again, Ben stood up, feeling both full and empty. He put on his gloves then left his money at the bar and walked away, hoping the men wouldn't make eye contact or try to speak to him. He kept his eyes on the door until he was back outside, where snow had begun to fall.

Chapter Four

"I wish to be left alone," said Scrooge. "Since you ask me what I wish, gentlemen, that is my answer. I don't make merry myself at Christmas."

~ Charles Dickens

CLEARING AWAY HER HUSBAND'S PORRIDGE bowl and coffee mug, Mary examined the scribbling again. *Gone out. Return soon. Ben.*

The note was a perfect reflection of what little she knew of the man—concise, direct, a bit curt, and completely mysterious. All the things he *didn't* say, things he didn't do, had her prickling with curiosity. And even George was inquisitive, as they'd speculated about Ben over breakfast minutes ago, going over all the obvious questions—where he came from, what he was running from, and who he used to be. She wondered if they would ever have any answers.

Hearing a soft knock, Mary set down the saucer and stepped toward the front door, realizing she was still in her dressing gown. She pulled on the knob and saw Ben in her doorway, looking significantly less rumpled than he had before. Something about his face was different. He'd trimmed his beard. His hair was cleaner, perhaps? *Hard to tell underneath that filthy cap...*

"Good morning." She stepped aside for him. "Come in and stand by the fire. Warm yourself," she insisted.

He dipped his head through the doorway, removed his cap and gloves, and made his way toward the fire.

"Thank you for the note," she continued. "I might've thought you'd left for good." She tried to insert a teasing tone in her voice, but she suspected it was lost on him. She shut the door and watched Bootsie circle Ben's shoes.

"That's why I left it. The note. Didn't want to concern you." He watched Bootsie sniffing at his trouser leg to assess exactly where he'd been.

Mary wondered, too, but she didn't dare ask.

Thoughtful and courteous, she thought, adding them to her growing list of traits that didn't seem to mesh with his gruffer side. The man was a walking paradox.

"Are you hungry? I have porridge," she offered, moving toward the kitchen.

"No, no. I've eaten. Thank you."

She noticed the flakes on his shoulders. "It's snowing again?"

"Only just. The cirrostratus clouds are hanging low..."

"Cirro...?"

"Snow clouds."

"Oh. Yes, which means we're in for a long, cold night."

He searched the ground for something else to say. "I think I'll retire for a bit."

"All right." She watched him leave in the direction of Sheldon's room.

She resumed her cleaning as Bootsie followed, meowing loudly for a treat. "You've had enough this morning, little one," she chided gently. "I'll not have a fat cat in this house."

He seemed to understand and changed his course. He leapt onto the sofa and kneaded the cushion with his paws.

Rinsing out the coffee cup with her hand, Mary hummed "O, Holy Night" and mused about how comforting it was to have another living, breathing human being in the cottage—even if that particular someone was an un-talkative, unkempt, utterly mysterious man who effortlessly used the word *cirrostratus* and slept most of the time. She didn't realize how lonely she got or how empty the cottage felt when George went to work. Having someone else only a couple of rooms away was a nice change.

Before she could rinse out the other mug, she heard another knock at the door and wished she had changed out of her dressing gown before breakfast. Combing down her short gray hair with her fingers, she knew her task was futile and gave up. Whoever was at the door would have to accept her as she was.

"Mrs. Pickering!" Mary said as she opened the door, her voice punctuated with surprise. "Please, come in."

Mary had only just seen Mrs. Pickering the day before. Odd that she should be at Mary's door, especially at 10:00 a.m., opening time. Mrs. Pickering should have been at the shop, manning her post, collecting gossip, and eavesdropping on customers. What was so important that she had to make an out-of-the-way house call?

"Good morning!" said Mrs. Pickering, bundled up in a taupe overcoat and matching scarf.

Mary shut out the cold and shivered. "May I offer you some tea?" she asked, knowing full well she would have to go to the trouble of putting the kettle on.

"No, I haven't time," Mrs. Pickering assured. "I only popped round to talk about the Dickens Festival, and the choir."

Something you could've done just as well by phone, Mary thought. Mrs. Pickering's eyes roamed about, searching the sofa and the floor for something specific.

"Are there problems?" Mary asked.

"Pardon?" asked Mrs. Pickering, forcing her gaze back to Mary.

"With the festival. Is something wrong?"

"Oh, no, no. Nothing of the sort. I was only wondering whether you'd be bringing the scones to this afternoon's rehearsal."

"Yes, of course." She'd told Mrs. Pickering as much yesterday, upon leaving her shop. "If the blizzard still allows us to *have* a rehearsal..."

Mrs. Pickering's eyes had taken to roaming again, and they stopped cold at Ben's leather jacket, which he'd apparently laid on the sofa before going into Sheldon's room. Mary panicked.

"Do you have a guest?" Mrs. Pickering stepped closer to the jacket. This wasn't about scones or the festival. Mrs. Pickering was on a blatant fact-finding mission, seeking exclusive information about "the stranger." Mary wondered how many other cottages she'd already inspected that morning, door-to-door.

"Uhm, no. I... that's George's jacket. Of course." She cleared her throat, hoping Mrs. Pickering wouldn't notice the enormous difference in size. George wore a small, while Ben probably wore an extra-large. But Ben's jacket lay crumpled so that the size was impossible to determine unless Mrs. Pickering dared to pick it up.

Mrs. Pickering's gaze lingered, as though considering the prospect, but suddenly, she turned and said, "Ahh. Well. Yes, the scones. All right, then. We're all set. I'm glad I stopped by to make sure. One can never be too diligent about the small things. Must be on my way to the shop." Moving toward the front door, she added, "Frightful weather predicted later today."

"Yes. Frightful." Mary let the cold in once again and wished Mrs. Pickering a good day. She wondered how long it would take before the entire village knew about Ben. The cat was surely out of the bag now.

Mary peeked out the window at the dreary sky. Thick snowfall threatened to create a challenging trek to the church hall. Snow was fine until she had to trudge out in it, get her ankles wet, and freeze her toes off. Still, the festival rehearsals were worth it, so she didn't give a second thought to bundling up and heading out.

"There you are." She saw Ben walking in from the bedroom, running a hand over his bearded chin with a yawn. "Did you sleep well?"

He nodded and rubbed his eyes. He resembled a little boy, vulnerable and disoriented from sleep. His hair seemed different to Mary. It was the same length—touching his shoulders—but it was cleaner and darker brown than she remembered from their first meeting.

"I was about to reheat some dumplings for you. I had a hunch you'd be up soon."

"You didn't need to do that." He approached the table.

"Nonsense. No trouble at all."

She moved to the kitchen and set the container in the microwave. As the airy hum started up, she peeked at Ben, saw him hunched at the table, and wondered what he was thinking. *Is he tired of being inside the cottage, staring at the same four walls?* Perhaps he needed a change of scenery.

"Ben, I have a proposition." She inched closer, knowing the response would be an instant no, but not caring. She pulled out the chair beside him, sat down, and threaded her fingers together on top of the table. "I'm going to a rehearsal. In fact, I'm nearly late for it. Anyway, I think you should come with me."

"Where?"

"The church hall, to the rehearsal. We're preparing for the annual Dickens Festival. I'm part of a group of twenty ladies who've formed a sort of caroling choir. On Christmas Eve, we'll walk around and sing throughout the village and then end with a concert inside the church. It's a lovely occasion. Don't you want to hear our rehearsal?"

He cocked his head, as if considering her proposal. His deep-set blue eyes searched the table. "I don't think I'd be very good company," he decided. A strand of hair fell near his cheek, and he didn't bother to brush it away. "Besides, look at me. I'm not exactly church ready."

"Nonsense. You look fine. They'll accept you as you are. Come along. Please? Honestly, I have a selfish motive—I'd love to have a bit of company on the walk. It's been snowing for hours now, and it might be a challenge for an old woman on icy ground. I have a bad back and arthritis, and I'll be carrying three boxes of scones from the bakery. I might fall and break a hip on the way! You wouldn't want *that* on your conscience." She thought she saw the corner of his lip curl up into an almost-smile. "You could sit at the back of the church," she continued. "No one will disturb you. I promise. You could be... well, my escort. My guardian."

The microwave beeped, and she supported her weight on the table to stand up slowly, her knees creaking and cracking. She went to stir the dumplings. The steamy vapors told her they were hot enough, so she found the thermos George sometimes took to work. After emptying the dumplings into it, careful to avoid splashes from the sauce, she reached for a spoon.

"Well," Ben mumbled, "I suppose a walk might do me some good."

"Perfect." She screwed the thermos lid on as tightly as her arthritis would allow then handed it to him. "I was hoping you'd say that. Here's your dinner. Transportable!"

She saw the quarter-smile grow, even heard the traces of a chuckle from his throat. It was a risk, but being presumptuous had paid off. She knew her own powers of persuasion. She tried not to use guilt trips often—only when they were absolutely necessary in twisting someone's arm a bit. *For their own good, of course.*

Mary's decision to invite Ben to join her had been so lightning quick that she'd forgotten his anonymity would be entirely exposed. People would see him walking with her in the street and immediately wonder who he was. The long hair and the beard would surely out him as "the vagabond." *But,* she reminded herself, *thanks to Mrs. Pickering's earlier visit and astute powers of observation, most people will already know the truth by now, anyway.*

People wouldn't mock him or talk about him to his face. No, the villagers were good at keeping those sorts of things to themselves, chattering over tea the next day in each other's parlors or sharing curious whispers while munching scones at the bakery:

"Did you see that scraggly man with Mrs. Cartwright?"

"Where did he come from?"

"He looks like a homeless person."

"Wonder how long he'll stay at the village. We'd best lock our doors."

No matter. Let them speculate. Let them gossip and titter and wonder. By the time the villagers started actively seeking answers, Ben would probably be long gone, off to another town, in search of whatever it was he couldn't find in Chilton Crosse.

Ben could have walked much faster than Mrs. Cartwright could, because of his much-longer legs and his youth. Still, he hovered slightly behind her, being patient as she plodded along on the pavement, shuffling through the snow at a snail's pace. The snowflakes caught in his eyelashes and buried themselves inside the collar of his not-warm-enough jacket.

Seeing how much farther the church was, he regretted coming at all. But his presence seemed important to Mrs. Cartwright—and he owed her his life. She was apparently the one who'd found him, facedown in the snow that evening. Something had caught her attention, made her look outside her window, call frantically to her husband, and get Ben the help he needed. The least he could do was accompany her—even at a snail's pace—to the other end of the village.

When they'd first set out, Ben had clutched the thermos, trying not to think about the dumplings inside. The omelet at the pub had satisfied him for a few brief hours, but when he'd awoken from his afternoon nap, he'd been famished again. He knew he could easily eat the thermos's contents in a few short gulps.

Mrs. Cartwright made a languid detour at the bakery, during which Ben traded his thermos for her three boxes of scones. He could smell hints of blueberry and cinnamon coming from the boxes' gaping seams. Ben continued following Mrs. Cartwright to the church at an even slower pace. Along the way, he noticed odd glances and lingering stares from passersby or people standing under shop awnings, probably wondering who the stranger was with one of their townsfolk. But what did he care? The people were strangers to him, too. Let them stare. He would be gone the next morning, anyway.

They finally reached the church, a modest, traditional old building with stained glass, thick-stoned arches, and a steeple. But Mrs. Cartwright bypassed the building and took a right, heading to the structure beside it. Ben juggled the boxes and reached his free arm out to open the door before she could get to it.

"Thank you, dear," she said as they stepped into a church hall, where a wall of warm air greeted them. Ben closed the door then followed Mrs. Cartwright inside the long room. At the far end stood a group of chattering ladies, and at the other, nearest Ben, stood a collection of tables and chairs pushed to the side.

Mrs. Cartwright removed her scarf and shook off the snow. "You can set the boxes here." She motioned to a table already filled with napkins, plasticware, a few covered dishes, and a couple of portable kettles.

"That might be a good spot for you," she whispered, pointing to a table in a dim area in the far corner, where the lights in the second portion of the hall weren't in use. She handed him the thermos, his reward.

Perhaps he could manage a bit of privacy, after all. She drifted off to meet up with the other ladies while he made his way to his temporary cave, eager to start on his dinner.

Ben removed his cap then his gloves, in order to unscrew the thermos lid. He took the first bite of dumplings. *Heaven.* A woman at the other end of the hall tapped a stick on the music stand in a futile attempt to attract the ladies' attention. Ben wondered how they got anything done. It seemed more like a social club gathering than choir practice. Mrs. Cartwright had joined them and stood in the center of the group, holding her music folder, ready to sing.

His second bite was as delicious as the first. Creamy goodness and tender chicken melted in his mouth. His mother used to make dumplings for him, ages and ages ago—always when he was ailing or sad. *Food for the soul,* she'd called it. On his third bite, he saw a figure approaching.

"Good evening," the man said, extending a shadowy hand. Ben caught the gleam of a white vicar's collar and swallowed that last bite the wrong way, which started him choking.

"Oh, I'm awfully sorry! I startled you." The vicar reached behind him for something as Ben tried his best to catch his breath. He coughed and cleared his throat, hoping to avoid making a scene and distracting the ladies in the choir. But their first song was well underway, and they were oblivious to him.

After a moment, Ben was able to swallow without coughing. The vicar handed him a paper cone filled with water, which he accepted. The cold water rushed down the back of his throat and made everything better.

"Cheers," Ben said, coughing a final time.

"No trouble at all." The vicar found a nearby chair and sat down.

Ben regretted taking the water, which had obligated him to enter into conversation. He had nowhere to hide.

"I'm Michael," the vicar said, extending his hand a second time.

Ben shook it, feeling the weight of social responsibility override his desire to flee the building.

Releasing the vicar's hand, Ben swallowed the rest of his water in one gulp, hoping his refusal to give his name would end the conversation before it began.

"Lots of snow out there." The vicar had begun the standard chitchat. *Weather. How original.* "We could get as much as eight inches, I'm told."

Ben studied him. Younger than any vicar he'd ever seen, Michael was in his mid-thirties, at best. With his boyish features, the man looked as if he were playing the role of a vicar, rather than actually performing the duties of one. Ben felt a little sorry for him. He was probably a genuinely nice person who meant well—he'd seen a stranger in a corner then attempted to be congenial, perhaps even win a soul. But Ben's was a soul not worth saving. And he wasn't in the mood to be patronized. The vicar wiped his hands on his thighs, brushing away imaginary lint, and tried again.

"So. Have you been in our fair village for long?"

"Not long." Ben returned to his dumplings.

"Ah. Well, you'll soon see how lovely the people are here." His voice, low and comforting, resonated the way a vicar's should. Ben wondered if the seminary offered special courses: "How to Speak Like a Vicar 101." He imagined a roomful of future vicars, repeating standard phrases and practicing their diction, their volume, and their tone.

"We're quite a welcoming place," Michael continued. "Lots of activities to offer. That is, if the snow doesn't engulf the whole village before nightfall." Chuckling at his own attempt at a joke, he folded his arms. "Will you be staying through the holidays with us?"

"No." Ben took another bite.

"I see. Well, I hope the time you *are* here will be restful for you. And that you find what you're looking for."

The vicar rose from his chair, and Ben peered at him again. *What would make him say such a thing to a stranger? Why would he assume I'm in search of anything? How incredibly presumptuous.*

"God bless you in your travels," the vicar said before leaving.

God. Ben had once been familiar with the concept. As a child, he'd stood sandwiched between his parents at a London cathedral, reading prayers in Latin. And during communion, he would dutifully accept a dry, tasteless wafer from a priest. *What did a wafer have to do with anything else?* he'd always wondered. *What mystery or world crisis did a wafer ever solve?*

Later, as a young adult released from the shackles of his parents' religion, he finally had the freedom, the choice to have God in his life. And he'd chosen not to. Sure, at first, Ben had told himself that he wasn't abandoning the Church—merely that other things were crowding out the need for it. Those things seemed far more important than Latin prayers, hymns, and empty symbols like crosses or wafers. Real-life, tangible things—such as education, girls, and creating a life that would even halfway live up to his father's standards—were the only things that mattered or made any sense to him.

But six months ago, the concept of God had turned from lukewarm to ugly. God had suddenly become a taker, a monster that removed any trace of good and stole it all away. God was the puppet master, watching His marionettes dance on a string at His will. At first, Ben had shaken his fist at Him, but after a while, his fist had grown tired. His anger was futile, anyway. God would do whatever God wanted to do. So why waste the energy?

Before long, Ben's anger had shifted to indifference, which had finally turned to atheism. Deciding not to believe at all made things easier. He had one less person to be angry with—one less thing in his life to distrust.

Ben finished his dumplings when the choir began the opening chords of "The First Noel." Feeling moody and restless, he reached for his gloves and hat again. But he had nowhere to go, and he couldn't abandon Mrs. Cartwright.

Puffing out an aggravated sigh, he sat back with a grunt, capped the empty thermos, and crossed his arms. *Why* had he agreed to come in the first place? He didn't belong there, amongst sweet little old ladies, vicars, and Christmas hymns that didn't move him. He belonged out there, in the cold, wandering and drifting like a snowflake.

Soon enough. He could certainly bide his time for a few more hours.

At 1:15 a.m., Ben heard Mrs. Cartwright click off her light and trudge down the hallway. After accompanying her back to the cottage hours earlier, Ben had claimed exhaustion and returned to Sheldon's room to sleep. But all he had done was wait—through Mr. Cartwright's late arrival home from work, through dinner and the muffled chitchat he could hear between them, through her knitting and his lingering at the fire until he finally turned in. But Mrs. Cartwright was a night owl and had lingered a little longer. Ben had quietly packed his bag then paced the bedroom floor. Finally, he'd given in and opened the book Mrs.

Cartwright had given him—a submarine novel he'd read before. He was halfway through it when he heard her light click off.

Sure, it would've been easier—and faster—to simply explain, say good-bye, then leave after the rehearsal. He could've gotten a nice head start with some daylight left in front of him. And he would have had to contend with a lot less snow. But something wouldn't let him face Mrs. Cartwright. He'd preferred to take the coward's way out and disappear in the middle of the night.

He waited beside the bedroom door, bag in hand, like a convict ready to escape. He could hear his own breathing, followed by the sound of Mrs. Cartwright's door closing. The coast was officially clear. He didn't feel the need to leave a note this time. They would see the empty room, his missing bag, the made bed. They would know he had moved on.

The hallway was dark, but fortunately, the fire in the sitting room cast a strong glow on the walls. Plus, the outside Christmas lights apparently winked all night long—he remembered them distinctly from the night he'd collapsed. They made colorful kaleidoscopes on the floor through the windows, cheerfully begging him to stay.

He reached for the front doorknob—nearly there!—then he heard something behind him.

"Leaving us?" Mr. Cartwright asked.

He'd been caught, royally. Ben swiveled to face Mr. Cartwright. He felt the need to explain, but all he could do was shrug.

Mr. Cartwright came closer, thrusting his hands into his pajama pockets. The fire's glow made his silver-peppered beard even more silver.

"Take care of yourself, son. I wish you the best."

"You're not going to talk me out of it?" Ben asked.

"I don't think I could."

Ben hadn't expected that. When he heard Mr. Cartwright's voice, he'd braced himself for a difficult good-bye, struggling to justify his getaway as if he were a thief in the night.

Sensing a sudden stab of gratitude and knowing it was his last chance to express it, he told Mr. Cartwright, "I can't thank you enough. For all you and your wife have done. Your kindness, your generosity..." Strong emotion bubbled up from his chest. He hadn't expected that, either.

40

"You're more than welcome, son. I'm only glad Mary was there to hear you fall. You would've died out there in the snow, otherwise."

Ben nodded and stared at the floor.

"Where will you go?" Mr. Cartwright asked.

"Not sure."

"I won't talk you out of leaving. But I will say this. You're welcome to stay through the holidays. I haven't heard you speak of any family, and this is the Christmas season. I know it would thrill Mary to bits, having you around. We'd both be glad to have you stay."

Ben glanced up to see the sincerity in Mr. Cartwright's eyes. He wasn't being a do-gooder, offering a handout to a weary traveler out of pity. He seemed to mean it.

"It's much too generous. I couldn't. I don't deserve that sort of... benevolence. You're better off letting me go."

"Nonsense. We'd love to have you stick around. No one should be alone on Christmas."

Ben saw the tree, lovingly decorated, beside the cozy fireplace. He thought of the dumplings, the warm bed, and the genuine hospitality. Then he thought of the alternative—wandering aimlessly in a snowstorm, shivering and hungry again. He had no idea how far the next village was or whether he would die before he even made it there. It was foolish not to at least consider the offer.

"I'd have to earn my keep," Ben insisted.

"I would expect nothing less. We could sort something out."

Ben paused, still not sure he was ready to commit to putting down roots, even shallow ones for a few weeks. "Only if you're certain..."

"I am," Mr. Cartwright said. "More than certain. And let's keep this little conversation to ourselves. Don't want the missus thinking you were trying to steal away without a good-bye. Wouldn't sit too well with her."

"Right."

"Now, I snuck out of bed for another helping of that plum pudding. Mary would disapprove, pat my stomach, and tell me a few extra pounds weren't worth the extra bites. So, I waited until she went to sleep. Silly woman, stays up all hours of the night. She's like a vampire."

Ben couldn't stop the grin.

41

"Care to join me?" Mr. Cartwright asked, already heading for the kitchen.

Realizing he hadn't eaten since the dumplings during the rehearsal, Ben said, "I'll be right there." He walked toward the bedroom to put his bag back where it belonged.

Chapter Five

It's enough for a man to understand his own business, and not to interfere with other people's.

– Charles Dickens

"WASN'T THAT A LOVELY SERMON?" Mary steadied herself on her husband's arm. "And a beautiful solo by Mrs. Wilkes. One of my favorite hymns."

"Mmm."

"And that dress she wore... she probably made it herself. That particular shade of green was so festive, wasn't it?"

"Mmm-hmm."

As they drew closer to the cottage, Mary hummed along to the faint piano music she heard drifting from somewhere. She'd never been more grateful to have her husband's solid frame supporting her. The "blizzard," which had really been no more than a few inches, had tapered off during the choir rehearsal the previous evening, and when Mary had awoken for church in the morning, the sun beamed happily, as though it had been doing so for days and days. Not that the snow on the ground had noticed—the still-cold temperatures had set it into hard, slippery patches, impossible to navigate without holding onto something sturdy, like one's husband.

Thank goodness the short walkway out of Mistletoe Cottage had been swept before Mary and George had stepped out for church.

"I meant to tell you earlier, how industrious it was of you, shoveling our walkway even before I got up! I was so impressed with you," Mary told George.

"That wasn't me," he said matter-of-factly.

Mary noticed his grin and squeezed his arm. "George Cartwright, do you mean to tell me that an elf or Father Christmas himself was responsible?"

"No. I think it was our new tenant, Ben."

"Tenant? Does that mean..."

"He's agreed to stay with us through the holidays." George gave a sidelong glance at his wife. "If that's all right with you, of course."

"It's wonderful!" She drew in an excited breath. "What made him change his mind and stay?"

"He didn't say, and I thought it best not to push him."

"Very wise of you, dearest. Yes, we mustn't press him about all the questions we have. He'll tell us in his own good time." She squeezed his arm again and turned her attention back to the cottage, all lit up, even in the bright sunlight. She couldn't bear to extinguish the lights, even in the daytime. "Where *is* that piano music coming from? Is it Mozart?" Mary tilted her head, trying to pinpoint the source of the melody.

George released his wife's arm to dig inside his pocket for the key to the cottage. When he opened the door, her question was answered. Ben sat at their piano, startled, fingers poised and frozen as he watched them enter. The music had stopped.

"Oh, that was beautiful! Don't quit on our account!" Mary exclaimed. "I didn't know you could play!"

Ben's cheeks flushed above his beard, and he reached up to close the keyboard's lid. "I'm sorry. I should've asked first."

"Don't be silly." She stood near him, at the piano's edge. "You're welcome to play anytime. In fact, I'm thrilled to hear it put to good use."

"Well, not sure about the 'good' part. I'm quite rusty."

"If that's rusty, I'd love to hear how you sounded in your prime," Mary gushed before realizing she was embarrassing him even more. "I inherited this piano from an old aunt a few years ago. It's sort of an heirloom."

"It's a respected brand," he admitted. "Nice, resonant tone. Needs a good tuning, though."

Mary chuckled. "Not surprising. I'm ashamed to admit—but do you know that it's never been played here in this cottage? Not once. Neither George nor I know how to play, but I couldn't bear to sell it.

44

I suppose I've used it as a sort of... decorative piece." She touched the smooth wood, straightened the fake snow, and righted a toppled ice skater. "This one's my favorite." She pointed to a man clutching the hand of a little girl. "I used to skate as a young girl. Those are the only clear memories I have of my father, when he laced up my skates and helped me wobble onto the ice." She realized she was rambling. "How long have you played?"

Ben rubbed his hands together. "Since I was a boy."

"Mary," George interrupted, "shall I help start the lunch?"

She saw right through him—George was trying to pull her away and distract her from Ben.

"Oh, all right." She walked toward the kitchen while removing her coat. "You cut the carrots, and I'll find the meat. How does a shepherd's pie sound to everyone?"

"Excellent!" Ben sounded more energetic than she'd ever heard him. He stood to follow her.

George took a handful of carrots then paused to focus on Ben. "You should know something. Apparently, you're an official member of the family now. Mary's long-lost nephew."

Confused, Ben looked to Mary for explanation. She giggled and threw up her hands. "I didn't know what else to say! We were at church, and Mrs. Pickering asked me point-blank in front of a cluster of choir members, *who* was the young gentleman at rehearsal with me yesterday? It just popped out—that you're my nephew, here for a visit. That appeased their curiosity, I think. But I lied. There, in the middle of church!"

She'd thought Ben might be upset, which was why she hadn't intended on telling him in the first place, but Ben's expression told her he approved. In fact, he seemed amused by the news.

"It's fine," he assured her. "I could do worse than being your nephew."

"Well, then, nephew. As you are part of this family, I'm putting you to work!" She handed him a peeler. "Oh, and call us Mary and George now. Wouldn't want to blow our cover, would you?" She winked.

Mary put him on potato-slicing duty, and before long, the three of them were working in different spaces of the kitchen. Meat sizzled, knives tapped against cutting boards, and Mary hummed the Mozart tune quietly. Soon, the pie was ready for assembly, which Mary decided to do alone.

"Too many cooks in the kitchen," she claimed, sending the men off to the sitting room to watch telly. George found an old Monty Python program on Channel 4, and from time to time, Mary heard soft chuckles, even from Ben.

It wasn't on the repairs list, but Ben knew how much it would mean to Mary. He'd spotted the gaps when he'd shoveled a thin layer of snow again at six o'clock Monday morning. Two red Christmas lights had gone out, and Ben was teetering on a ladder, trying to unscrew and replace them. Gloves had made the task even more difficult, so he had removed them, exposing his fingers to the cold. He'd seen some replacement lights in a drawer the day before, while searching for a hammer. Naturally, the dead lights stood far apart—on opposite sides of the roof. Rather than grumble, he decided it was a miniscule price to pay for being given shelter, food, and kindness.

"Need a hand?" a Scottish-accented voice called from below.

Ben screwed in the light with a final twist before gingerly shifting his weight to peer down. He saw the silver-haired man from the pub— Mac. He was looking up at Ben, squinting into the sunlight and holding a toolbox. A thick rope encircled his shoulder and arm.

Ben climbed down, careful to distribute the weight of his boots on the thin ladder steps, then reached the snow with a crunch.

"Thanks, no. Just finished up." Ben found the glove inside his pocket and slipped it back on.

"Mac MacDonald." He offered his own gloved hand.

"Ben Granger." He caught Mac's hand in a lively shake and saw the hint of a cordial smile beneath the stubbled jaw.

Mac had gray-blue eyes that turned the otherwise-rough edges of his face softer and friendlier. Even so, Ben knew what came next—that uncomfortable part of any new conversation in which nosy people sized up other people and gathered information about them. Though Mac didn't *seem* the nosy type...

"Quite a job, Christmas lights." Mac observed Ben's handiwork.

"Indeed. Replacing them can be tedious," Ben replied, not knowing what else to say. "Looks like you're off to a job, yourself." He gestured toward the toolbox.

"Aye. Mr. Lattimer's van."

"Oh. I'd thought you were a plumber. I mean, well, at the pub that day..."

"Aye. I dabble in a bit of everything. Repairs, landscaping, plumbing, automobiles. Whatever's needed. Mac-of-all-trades, you could say."

Ben grinned at the pun, though Mac's face remained the same: deadpan. He was full of surprises, this one.

"Are you looking for work, son? I could use a hand now and again. If you're interested."

Caught off-guard, Ben paused, longer than he'd intended. "Err... well..."

"Think it over. You can reach me here." Mac pulled a business card from his coat pocket and handed it to Ben. "I finally got a mobile phone—early Christmas present from my granddaughter. Guess she was tired of not being able to reach me." He chuckled.

And with a nod of his cap, he was off.

"Thanks," Ben called after him then flipped the card over. Sparse and to the point, the card displayed only Mac's name and landline number in a plain black font. His new mobile number was penciled in below that.

Ben tucked the card inside his pocket, reached for the ladder, and hoisted it away from the roof with ease. It had been a few days since his collapse, and he was mostly recovered. The headaches and shakes were gone, as well as the constant lethargy that had hung over him like a dense cloud. He felt more energetic than he had in many weeks.

Lugging the ladder around to the small garden shed behind the cottage, Ben was aware of how tense he'd been with Mac, preparing to cover his tracks and lie should Mac start digging. Surely he'd heard the rumors around the village: a mysterious nephew, a wanderer collapsing in the street, the scraggly-bearded man suddenly appearing in their fair village and taking refuge in the Christmassy cottage.

Opening the shed with one hand and balancing the ladder with the other, Ben realized he hadn't thought everything through. Even staying a few short weeks had consequences. Sooner or later, he would have to open up, to offer a little information about himself, at least to the Cartwrights. People expected that sort of thing. But he couldn't stay cooped up inside Mistletoe Cottage for days on end.

He would have to venture out now and then and face people's questions. Thank goodness that, for the time being, Mac hadn't been one of those people.

"That'll be thirteen pounds, even." Mary placed the hardcover novel into a brown paper bag. She took Mrs. Harrison's money and wished her a happy Christmas. Mary always enjoyed being able to tell something about people by the books they bought for themselves: historical romance for Lizzie Tupman, architecture books for Adam Spencer, and the Bronte sisters for Gertrude Middleton.

"Here they are." Holly approached the register and handed over the new books. Mary examined all three covers—a gun with bullet holes, a police badge, and a mysterious passport. The book titles were all stamped in bold, masculine fonts.

"Yes," she said. "These will do just fine."

"Did your nephew enjoy the last one, the submarine novel?"

"Nephew? Oh, yes. Ben. I believe he did. He finished it in three days' time."

"Those action books are fast reads. Or so Fletcher tells me. Not really my thing." Holly shrugged. "But that's the beauty of books, isn't it? Everyone gets to choose the world they want to live in for three hundred pages or so."

"Indeed. Oh! Speaking of—when does the new book club start up again?"

"I thought we could wait until right after the holidays. Things get so busy for people around this time, it would be a challenge to have full attendance. I think we'll meet the first week of January."

"At Gertrude's cottage?"

"At her insistence."

"How wonderful. And it's *Little Women*?"

"Yes. I thought it would be a slight departure from Jane Austen.

Though I had to quarrel with Gertrude about it. She's such an Austen fan now that she insisted on having the book club read all six books, back-to-back. But I thought we needed a little break in the middle. We'll get back to Austen soon. I had to promise. So, in the end, she caved. *Little Women*, it is."

"I haven't read that book since I was a wee girl," Mary said with fondness. "I think I even still have my old copy, though it's frail and falling apart. Should be interesting, reading it again through adult eyes."

"My thoughts exactly." Holly placed the new books into a bag for Mary. "Those childhood books tend to stay with us, don't they?"

"They certainly do. Thank you again for these. If you need me longer, I might be able to stick around..."

"No, it's fine. There's a lull. And anyway, Rosalee is coming in half an hour for her shift."

"Well, in that case, I'll leave you to it."

Mary hugged the package to her chest and prepared herself for the blustery winds that stirred up the snow into miniature cyclones outside the window.

Five minutes later, she opened her cottage door to the familiar, hearty scent of shepherd's pie. Shutting the door, she saw Ben, lifting a portion of steaming pie onto a plate. He glanced up and gave a sheepish smile.

"Hope you don't mind. Thought I'd warm up the leftovers."

"Of course I don't mind," said Mary, walking closer. "It was thoughtful of you."

Something was different. As she approached, she saw that Ben's beard was gone! The hair was the same length but combed through. He was a new man. A younger man.

"You shaved!" she exclaimed, setting down the books. Their weight had felt more like ten books than three by the time she'd reached the cottage.

"Yes." He reached for a second plate. "Got tired of the itching."

Mary removed her scarf and chuckled. "I wish you'd talk George into shaving his. I keep telling him he'd look twenty years younger without it. And his kisses wouldn't be so scratchy."

"I don't know that I could change his mind." Ben focused on the pie, careful not to drop any bits on the table as he transported it from pan to plate. "A man's beard is a sacred thing. Or so I'm told. It's the first time I've ever had one."

She studied his face while he wasn't looking—his chin, the strong line of his jaw, the thin-ish lips. He had a handsome face, not rugged but still masculine. She would need a while to get used to the new man standing in her kitchen, doling out portions of shepherd's pie.

"Oh," she said, remembering. "These are for you. I exchanged the Campbell book for them—you were finished with it, weren't you?"

"Yes." He set down the spatula, reached inside the bag, and removed the three books in one grasp. As he sorted through them, he would pause, flip the book to skim the back cover, nod, and move to the next. She hoped the nods meant approval.

"Haven't read these before." He glanced up. "Thank you. But really, it's too generous…"

"Not at all." She struggled out of her coat. "Holly Newbury—that's the bookshop's owner—has a used-books section and said she'll just shelve them there when I return them. Didn't cost me a single pence."

Ben came around the table to help her out of her coat. "Nice of her to do that."

"She's wonderful. Our little librarian, I call her. She began a book club over the summer that made readers out of everyone. I love working at her shop. Well, volunteering, more like. Most people would hate working retail during a bustling holiday season, but I rather enjoy it. Especially when I get to hear good news first-hand—"

"News?" He picked up the spatula, finished plating Mary's portion, then slid it to her side of the table as she sat down.

"The best news. Bobby Cahill—only son of our local veterinarian— is only eight years old. Adorable little boy with ginger hair and sparkling green eyes. Well, he was diagnosed with leukemia earlier this year. I was wondering why Bobby wore so many ball caps and why he looked so pale. I knew he was ill but never imagined leukemia. The parents decided to keep it a secret until a few weeks ago. They're very private people."

"Understandable. A leukemia diagnosis can be devastating. Some people like to hunker down, keep things in the family."

"Yes, true," she agreed as Ben joined her at the table. "Anyway, Bobby's had a blood transfusion and several months of chemotherapy, bless his brave little heart. The parents took him to a hospital in Bath for treatments and testing. Well, today, the vet, his wife, and Bobby all came into the bookstore with these enormous smiles. Bobby announced to everyone—he's in remission!"

"That's excellent. Children can often fight the disease better than adults. He'll still have to be watched carefully for the next few years, but remission is the best possible outcome."

Mary wondered how Ben knew so much about the disease. Perhaps a family member or friend of his had suffered from it. "Yes. There was a collective shout of joy from all of us standing there. And, precious boy, all he could talk about after that was his insatiable desire for a trip to Disney World. He even wore little mouse ears and showed them off proudly. The mother kept patting his shoulder and saying, 'We'll see.' I highly doubt his parents can afford that sort of trip, especially with all the costs of treatment. But I'm sure they'll find a way."

"No doubt. They deserve a nice break after what they've been through."

"Indeed." Mary shifted her focus to her food. "I didn't realize how hungry I was until this very minute. George will be missing out, but I can reheat his when he returns. He plays poker once a week at the bakery. They close up shop early for it—Old Mr. Bentley's idea, began years ago. It became so popular, they started rotating in the newer members. Even the vicar joins them, when he's able."

"The vicar? Gambles?"

"Well, I wouldn't call it gambling, exactly. It's quite harmless. They play with plastic tokens," she confided then shook her head. "I don't see the fun in that. But I can't fault George for his poker nights. He doesn't see the fun in my book club or choir rehearsals, but he never complains. I'd be a hypocrite to nag at him to stay home. Nothing worse than a hypocrite..." She dug her fork into the first bite. "Mmm. Every bit as good as the day it was made, don't you think?"

He nodded his agreement as he took his first bite.

"People underestimate leftovers. I'm a fan of them. Takes a few quick minutes to heat them, and there you have it. No waste, no want."

"Drinks," Ben said suddenly, with a click of his finger, and got up to fetch them.

"Water is fine. Don't go to any trouble for me," she called after him.

He returned with two water glasses and set them down.

They clinked forks against the plates and ate in silence until a thought popped into Mary's head. "May I ask you a question?" she ventured, since he seemed in good spirits.

Ben hesitated then shrugged his okay.

"I want to know more about your musical background. When I heard you playing the piano—well, I can recognize talent. You certainly must have been schooled..."

Ben dipped his head, and she couldn't tell whether it was because of humility or embarrassment. He wiped his mouth and took a swig of water.

"A long time ago," he said softly, his gaze returning to another place and time, "music was my passion. I took to it immediately, at four years old—became obsessed with the piano in our parlor. Something about pressing the keys and hearing notes emit from a wooden box fascinated me. Mum enrolled me in theory lessons, piano lessons. She was only humoring me, but I was dead serious. Wanted to become a concert pianist someday..."

"And did you?"

"Oh, no." He plunged his fork into a mound of mashed potato. "Father didn't approve. So I went into what you might call the 'family business.' By the time he'd lectured me into thinking music was an empty, unreachable goal, I had started to believe him. And that was that." His clipped tone told Mary he didn't want to discuss it further.

She cleared her throat and returned to her meal. "Families are funny things," she mused. "Expectations, obligations, duties that they attach to one another. A relative's opinion matters so much. Too much, I sometimes think..." She realized she was rambling, probably boring him to tears. "In any case, your path has led you here, to our doorstep. And I'm glad of that."

She meant every word, but he probably thought of her as a silly old woman, overemotional or melodramatic. *Time for a change of subject.* "We're almost ready for dessert. Interested in a scone? Maybe a custard tart?"

"No. Thank you." He rose to gather his plate and utensils.

She crisscrossed her own fork and knife over her nearly empty plate and followed him to the kitchen. "I'll take those," she insisted as he switched on the tap. "You cooked. I'll wash up."

"Fair enough, thanks. I think I'll retire early." He collected his new books from the table.

"Have a good rest," she called after him, thankful for their brief talk. Still, Mary wondered if her prodding had been too much, too soon. She hoped he wouldn't retreat into his shell again. Oddly, hearing those new bits of information had only made her more curious than ever. The pieces in this puzzle still weren't fitting.

There was more to his story; she was sure of it. She only hoped she had enough time to discover it.

Chapter Six

Figures passed and repassed there; and the hum and murmur of voices greeted his ear sweetly.

~Charles Dickens

B EN, IN HIS FORMER LIFE, had always been enslaved to time. He would set three alarm clocks each evening and consult two day planners each day, and he never, ever left home without a watch precisely synchronized to the clock in his car.

But the past few weeks had been a colorless blur. Days ran together, one after the next. In fact, Ben had taken off his timepiece the night before and tucked it into a pocket inside his bag. Somewhere along his journey, the watch had stopped ticking, anyway. During his wandering, before he'd collapsed outside Mary's cottage, his hours had held no shape or form. Time had become irrelevant. But lately, he experienced that pull again for a bit of structure, the desire for a point of reference, at least, at which hours actually meant something.

That desire was further strengthened by the nightmare that had rattled him out of sleep an hour ago. He'd awoken with an erratic jerk, his heart thumping and palms sweating. The nightmare always held the same vivid images—black umbrellas glossy with rain, a red handkerchief, and a steady beep gone silent. The suffocating cloud of the dream had settled over him and remained long after he'd forced himself out of bed, brushed his teeth, and combed his hair.

Restless, Ben walked into the sitting room and felt the stabbing in his abdomen. He hadn't had pain for a couple of days, leading him to hope that healing was already taking place. But maybe it wasn't.

He went in search of antacids, and on the way, he read the note

Mary had placed on the table: *Gone to choir rehearsal. Be back around noon. Make yourself breakfast.* Ben glanced at the to-do notepad beside it, hoping George had added something before leaving for work. But the pad was entirely blank. Ben was on his own for the day.

He found the tablets and struggled to swallow them without any water. Then the wooden advent calendar caught his eye. Walking toward it, near the front window, he saw the date of the last opened door—the eighth day of December. He'd been in Chilton Crosse for eight days. Was that possible? Certainly, that was the longest he'd spent time in one place since he'd quit his job four—no, five—weeks ago. Even now, after finding a comfortable rhythm—keeping up with regular hygiene, reading nearly all the books Mary got him, feeling useful by helping out around the cottage—he still had the consistent urge to chuck his things into his bag, scrawl out a quick note, and walk out the door forever. But a voice inside told him to fight it.

Maybe it was that same voice reminding him about Mac's card. Ben needed something to fill the time, a bigger distraction than small tasks inside the cottage. He went to his jacket on the coat rack and reached inside the pocket then walked toward the kitchen phone, card in hand. He dialed, having no idea what he would actually say once Mac answered.

"Hello?" he heard on the other end.

"Err... hi. Hello. Mac? This is Ben. Ben Granger."

"Oh, aye. The Cartwrights' nephew."

"Yes. I, uhm, I was wondering if you needed... if you had extra work for me? I'm free this morning. Actually, I can give you the entire day. If you need me, that is."

"I can always use an extra hand, aye."

"You should know," Ben confessed, "I'm not very good. At handyman things. I'm not a carpenter or repairman. But I am a quick study."

"That's all you need, a sharp mind. The hands will follow. 'Tis what my grandfather always told me."

Some of Ben's confidence returned. "Well, if you're willing, I'm available."

"Can you meet me at Elton's farm? About a half mile north of the village, off the main road. Can't miss it."

"I'll be there in fifteen minutes."

Oddly, suddenly, the dread shifted into a small rush of excitement. New work *was* an escape, of sorts, venturing into the unknown. He had no idea what to expect from the day. He was in Mac's hands. And for whatever reason, he knew he could trust that.

Chopping wood in chilly weather left Ben with the odd sensation of being hot and cold at the same time. The sweat on his brow turned cold, and icy air brushed his skin each time he swung his ax, finally forcing him to remove his jacket. He'd become quite good at chopping wood and soon picked up the pace. He'd never swung an ax before in his life. He'd never had reason to, city boy that he was. But he could see the satisfying appeal of hard labor, of channeling one's emotions and energies into striking something as hard as one could. It also required little logic and brainpower. He could switch over to autopilot: grab the wood, place it steady on the block, swing the ax at an angle, split the wood, toss it aside, then reach for another piece.

While Ben chopped, Mac had gone to do repairs on a barn at the opposite end of the farm. Mr. Elton was getting too old to do the necessary work, and so Mac lent a hand now and again, to lighten the load.

"I see you've made progress," Mac said when he returned. His work boots made zigzag patterns in the few bits of snow the sun hadn't melted.

Ben was mid-swing and out of breath, and after he chopped the piece, he set the ax aside, grateful for a break. He could already feel the stiffness in his back and shoulders. Tomorrow's soreness would be hellish.

"Nearly finished with the load," Ben assured.

"Good timing. We're due at the church in an hour. I'll treat you to a pub lunch beforehand."

"The church, eh?" Ben squinted in the sunlight. He had a quick choice to make: risk seeing the vicar, which meant he might be interrogated or preached at, or make up a solid excuse to return to the cottage, where he could skulk about, feeling like a useless coward.

"Aye, Michael wants decorations put up. 'Tis usually my job to do it. And perhaps some minor repairs done, as well." Mac waited patiently for Ben's answer.

Integrity won out. Ben needed to live up to his offer of a full day's work. Plus, he remembered his ulcer and knew a meal would help. An empty stomach would only make his condition worse. "Sounds fine. Let me finish these last pieces. Won't take a minute."

At the pub, Mac introduced Ben to the man behind the bar. "This is Joe, himself. Owner of this fine establishment."

Joe chuckled and gave a sort of eye roll.

Mac ignored him and continued. "Joe, this is Ben Granger. He's nephew to Mary Cartwright."

Guilt pricked Ben's conscience over letting the lie continue. But it wasn't his lie. What else could he do but go along? Correcting the lie would expose Mary and taint her reputation. Surely, the ruse was harmless enough, in the end.

"Nice to meet you!" Joe said, offering a hearty handshake across the bar. "Mary's nephew, eh? Whereabouts are you from?"

"London. Well, originally. Been moving around a lot lately, though."

"Sounds like an exciting life. You two have a seat, and I'll get you started. Everything on the house. A proper welcome-to-the-village lunch!"

Later, at the corner table, Mac munched on his fish and chips in silence while Ben sipped his potato soup. He'd wanted to order something hearty, ribs or cottage pie, as Mac had. But the soup would be better for his ulcer, so Ben had caved.

He sat back and stretched his long legs under the table, reaching for a sip of water. "I wanted to thank you," he told Mac, who had tipped another chip to his mouth.

"For what, son?" He popped it in and munched.

"For taking me on such short notice. Without even knowing me. Not asking for references or past experience."

Mac gave a nod and focused on his food. His voice raspy and weathered, he said, "'Tis not my business to pry into other folks' affairs. I figure if they wish to tell me about themselves, they will. In time."

He looked up into Ben's eyes without blinking, still chewing, then looked down again.

All of Ben's concerns had been moot—the vicar was nowhere to be seen when Ben and Mac arrived at the church. Mac mentioned something about him visiting an ailing parishioner. Mac and Ben spent the whole of the afternoon stringing white lights and decorating trees inside the church hall. Then later, they added poinsettias and white candles to the sanctuary.

At the end of the workday, Mac tried to pay him, but Ben refused. He might be able to perpetuate the lie of being someone's nephew, but he wasn't about to take Mac's money when he had more than enough sitting in the bank. So, rather than say he didn't "need" the money, Ben made up some excuse about the hard work being payment enough. Mac didn't question him further.

By the time Ben reached Mistletoe Cottage, night had fallen. He got a whiff of himself before he reached the door. He cringed at the odor—sweat mixed with a faint scent of fried fish, leftover from the pub. He was in dire need of a bath.

He knocked softly then reached for the knob, figuring Mrs. Cartwright—*Mary*, he remembered—wouldn't mind if he walked on in.

"*There* you are," she exclaimed, taking off her glasses. She was sitting in her rocking chair near the fire, a long stretch of navy-blue fabric across her lap. "I was about to call out the search party!"

"Blast. I forgot to leave a note." He grimaced. "Sorry about the language." He closed the door. Every movement took effort. His body, head to toe, ached with the efforts of hard labor. But it was a good ache. A worthy ache. "I should've rung you, but we got so busy—"

"We?"

"Oh. Mac MacDonald. Since Mr. Cartwright—"

"George," she corrected.

"Right. Since George didn't have any work for me today, I rang Mac. He'd said he needed an extra pair of hands for the holidays."

Mary put aside her sewing. "You don't have to explain. I was only teasing about the search party. You know you're welcome to come and go as you please. I'm glad you had such a nice, long day out. Fresh air. Good for the lungs." She stood and smoothed out her beige skirt. "Are you hungry?"

"A bit," he confessed. "But I'm in greater need of a good bath. Don't come near—I'm afraid you'd pass out from the stench."

She chuckled. "I doubt that. But you go ahead with your bath, and I'll make you a snack."

"Where's Mister... where's George?" he asked.

"Went to bed early. He claims the flu, but I think it's only allergies." She lowered her voice to a whisper. "He's a bit of a hypochondriac, you know."

"Ah." Ben headed down the hall, so tired that he nearly forgot to dip his head under the doorframe and came within two centimeters of giving himself a horrible headache.

Half an hour later, after a bath, nothing sounded better than a lie-down by the fire. His mind was too revved up to sleep, but his muscles begged to recline. He entered the sitting room, dressed in a freshly laundered flannel shirt and jeans, his hair still damp. Mary had bought him sleepwear—"proper pajamas," she'd called them—but he didn't feel comfortable wearing them about the cottage. He would change into them later.

The moment his body dropped onto the sofa beneath him, his every muscle relaxed. For the first time in ten hours, he closed his eyes and felt the tension drain away. He didn't think he could ever move again.

"Here you are," Mary said, approaching his side.

It took everything in him to move to a sitting position, to command his torso and limbs to cooperate.

"Thank you," he said, as she handed him a big steaming bowl of... potato soup.

"I made it this afternoon. Thought it would make for a nice evening meal. Comfort food."

"It's perfect." He ate quietly as she returned to her rocking chair and picked up the blue fabric.

"This is for the Dickens Festival," she told him. "Twenty costumes, all to be hemmed. Of course, I'm not hemming *all* twenty." Her fingers moved nimbly, knowingly. The needle popped in and out of the fabric so quickly that it barely registered to the eye, past a thin flash of metal. "I'm only responsible for seven. But seven is enough, with a petticoat this wide." She lifted the fabric and showed him the enormous circle that cascaded onto the floor.

"Blimey," he said through a sip of soup.

"I love it, I admit. Even with all the hard work involved. Nothing like a festival to make things seem Christmassy..."

"Does it happen every year? The festival?" he asked, finishing off the last spoonful.

"Every *couple* of years or so," she said, gently rocking. "It's such a big production, we have to give ourselves a break. Of course, one Christmas tradition that doesn't take a break is our Mystery Claus. We see him every year. Well, not really 'see' him. Nobody's *ever* seen him."

"Mystery Claus?" Ben asked.

"Yes. Well, I assume it's a 'him.'" She placed her hands in her lap, still holding the needle, and removed her glasses. She leaned in, as if the walls had ears. "It's like having our own Father Christmas. For the past twenty years, at least, someone—a person from the village, I assume—has left presents on certain folks' doorsteps. Not random doorsteps, mind you. It's very deliberate. Only those in need. Folks who have just lost a job or someone who's had a tragedy the year before. Usually people with broken spirits, broken lives."

"Interesting."

"And eerie. This person knows details about the village. He's very specific with the gift-giving—only gives people exactly what they need. Age-appropriate toys for children—the exact number inside the household, in fact! Or maybe an expensive wheelchair for an elderly person. One year, he even placed a new dishwasher on the porch of someone whose washer had broken the month before. Imagine that!"

"Amazing."

"And the money it would take for that each year? Goodness, it's staggering. Thousands of pounds, over the years. We all have our own theories, mind you. I tend to think that Mrs. Pickering might be involved. She owns the grocer's, and she knows everyone in the village, all our personal details. It would make sense. But then, she would need help, wouldn't she? Moving the items, especially the heavy ones, transporting them to the cottages, then placing them on doorsteps. Another possibility is Dr. Andrews. He has the financial means. And a heart of gold. Or Duncan Newbury, richest man in town." She paused and shook her head. "Imagine this. Once upon a time, I even suspected my own husband! George is acquainted with everyone in the village. He's aware of their problems and difficulties. But it would be impossible for him to hide it from *me* all these years. And, of course, we're not wealthy enough. Unless he has a secret stash somewhere he's been keeping from me..."

Though genuinely interested in the mystery person, Ben craved relief—his sore body needed a soft place to fall. His hands had even started to shake during the last couple of minutes as he'd held the bowl. Rather than let it fall and break, he set it on the floor and carefully lay back on the sofa with a grunt, closing his eyes.

"Oh, I'm sorry. You must be knackered," Mary said. "I'll stay quiet. Let you rest."

"No, it's fine. I'm only shutting my eyes. Go on."

Somewhere between talk of the Father Christmas mystery and the next day's weather, Ben's mind fell into an abyss of beautiful, airy unconsciousness as he gave in to luscious sleep.

Chapter Seven

As I hope to live to be another man from what I was, I am prepared to bear you company, and do it with a thankful heart.

~Charles Dickens

THE PAGES TURNED LIKE TISSUE paper. Always afraid she would rip them—and she had, a few times before—Mary handled them with a sensitive touch. George often prodded her to purchase a new Bible, but she couldn't bear the thought. The book had been her grandmother's, with underlined passages that had been important to her decades before and notes scrawled in the margins from her vicar's sermons. Most people would've treated the Bible as a delicate heirloom, something to be placed on the shelf, dusted often, and taken down once a year for a Christmas reading. But Mary put it to use, reading out of it nearly every day. It had helped her in her very darkest of days, thirteen years before, and she'd made a habit of looking to its wisdom ever since. Even the simple act of placing it in her lap and feeling its weight gave her a familiar comfort.

Because of the holiday season, she was reading the Christmas story. Normally, she read from one of the four Gospels about Jesus's birth. But today, she decided to go further back, to Isaiah, to the prophecy. She hummed along to the melody in her head of Handel's "Messiah" as she read the words: "For unto us, a child is born..."

She heard footsteps and looked up to see Ben shuffling into the room. He walked as if he were a hundred years old.

"Did the heating pad help?" she asked, wincing along with him.

"A bit." He walked closer, his hand cradling his lower back. "Sorry. I've interrupted you."

"No, it's fine. I'm doing my daily reading."

"Which book?" he asked then saw the Bible.

"Well, I typically bounce around, see where things take me. But this month, it's the Christmas story. I'm reading a passage in Isaiah—I'm sure you know it well enough, with your musical background." She didn't dare sing, but she quoted by heart: "'And the government shall be upon his shoulders. And he will be called Wonderful Counselor, Mighty God, Everlasting Father, Prince of Peace...'"

"Isaiah 9:6," he rattled off.

"Yes." She was impressed.

He scratched at his jaw, where a hint of stubble had grown overnight. "As you said, I know it from a musical standpoint..."

"Ah. Well, I was about to flip to my favorite part." She thumbed carefully until she reached the spot, a few pages over.

Her peripheral vision caught him shifting his balance and putting a hand into his jeans pocket—a sure sign of either boredom or discomfort. Still, she pressed on.

"It's Isaiah, Chapter Fifty-three. Most people don't realize how this relates to Christmas, but it really does. It details who Christ became. And why He arrived here..."

Ben probably felt stuck, having to listen to her wee sermon, but he had asked what she was reading, and that was her answer. Besides, her faith was a part of her. Over the past several days, she'd shown Ben many other sides of who she was. Why not this part, as well?

"Here." She began to read a verse, but before she could even get the first few words out, Ben interrupted.

"May I ask you..." He settled on the arm of the sofa across from her.

"Mmm?"

"Well. I hate to sound impudent. But... do you really believe all that?" He waved a pointed finger toward the book she held.

"What? The Bible?"

"Well, yes. Things such as a virgin birth. Or a resurrection. Or a giant whale spitting out a man..."

"Absolutely. Don't you?"

Ben ran a hand through his long dark hair. "If I'm truthful, no. There was a time I used to. As a boy. Not anymore."

63

Mary hadn't expected that. The topic was such a fragile one, much like the paper she held between her fingers. With a single misstep, a wrong word spoken, their conversation could be torn in two and change their entire relationship. She might fracture whatever it was they'd built.

"What made you stop believing?" she heard herself ask. "If you don't mind my asking."

Ben shook his head, but his answer was slow, thoughtful. His eyes skimmed the stone floor as he spoke. "Lots of things, I suppose, over the years. I think it started at university, being exposed to education, liberal thought. Philosophy classes widened my perspective, made me look outside the rote I'd been taught in Mass. Then, as an adult, I saw the bigger world issues, bigger than myself. The cruelty of how some people are made to live, things they have to endure. Where is God in all of that? Why doesn't He reach out and stop it, if He's all-powerful?" He shifted and softened his expression, clearly trying to balance his honesty with tact, for her sake. "Then, not long ago, it became quite a personal reason…" He paused, and just as he'd decided to open his mouth again to finish his sentence, the phone rang.

Planning to let the answerphone pick it up, Mary remembered the call she was expecting from Mrs. Pickering about the next rehearsal. The mood was already broken anyway. Ben stood with a deep breath, visibly relieved by the interruption.

"I should probably get that," she muttered, attempting to get up from the rocking chair quickly enough—but her creaking knees wouldn't allow it.

"Want me to answer it?" Ben offered, moving toward the phone.

"Yes. Please. And remember—you're my *nephew*." She winked. "Should anyone ask."

He caught it on the fourth ring. "Cartwright residence."

Mary was plodding toward the phone, but she paused when she heard Ben say, "Oh, hello… yes, certainly… all right…"

She stared out of curiosity until he hung up the phone.

"That was for me, actually. Mr. MacDonald," Ben explained, pointing a thumb back to the phone. "He's got another job for me today. If that's okay. I already repaired your toilet's latch and replaced a couple of lightbulbs when I woke up this morning. I don't think I had anything else from George left to do."

"No, of course it's fine. But your back…"

Ben shrugged as George had many times, brushing Mary off whenever she showed a bit of concern for his health. "It'll be fine," he said. "Doesn't sound as if there's any hard labor planned for me today."

"Well, that's good."

"What do you know about him? Mac? I have trouble reading him sometimes. Seems like a bit of an enigma."

Mary nearly chuckled as Ben stood in front of her, the very definition of the word *enigma*.

Seeing that Ben hadn't caught the irony, she tried to answer his question with a straight face. "Mac can be a bit mysterious, yes. I know he was once married long ago, has a daughter, I think, and perhaps a granddaughter or two? But they don't live here. He's been here in the village as long as I can remember, working around the fringes of it, always helping out whenever we need him. He's the heart and soul of this place, if you ask me. As fine a man as they come."

"He seems genuine. Hard-working."

"That's for sure. I don't think I've ever seen him rest, as a matter of fact," Mary admitted. "Well, I was going to offer you a hearty lunch, but it seems you have a busy day ahead."

"Mac and I will grab a late lunch mid-day, I'm sure." Ben found his jacket. "I won't be back until dark, most likely."

"Have a lovely day, Ben."

"You, as well." He waited for her to make eye contact again, then he said, "I hope I didn't offend you. Before the call. Being so blunt about my beliefs. Or lack thereof." He grinned. "That was never my intent—to offend."

"No offense taken at all. You're entitled to your beliefs. Or lack thereof."

His smile grew into a grin, and she even heard a chuckle as he turned to go.

The cottage seemed suddenly very empty, even as Bootsie remained at the door and meowed his good-bye. He'd become quite attached to

Ben and had taken to following him around the cottage, even scratching at his bedroom door early each morning.

Mary mused about their earlier conversation, wondering what personal story he'd been about to tell her when the phone interrupted. She hoped that, one day soon, he might finish it...

Ben zipped his jacket after closing the cottage door, grateful not to have to trudge through—or shovel!—fresh snow. Everything had melted away, leaving him a rather pleasant walk to Mac's cottage.

On the way, he chided himself for letting his guard down with Mary. He'd never intended to inquire after her faith or give that much information about his beliefs. He didn't know where all the God talk had come from. But he couldn't take it back. It was out there for her to ponder and analyze. He hoped she wouldn't press him on it later, that she would forget he had said anything at all.

Forcing his mind elsewhere, he thought about his day. On the phone, Mac had mentioned something about a "commissioned" project involving carpentry. That sounded intriguing—and intimidating. The only experience he'd ever had was nailing pictures to a wall or using an occasional screwdriver.

He reached Mac's cottage within minutes and noticed how well it represented the character of its inhabitant. A humble, unassuming stone cottage with a thatched roof, the house sat on the outskirts of the village, over a hill. In fact, it was isolated from the main street and the other buildings. It sat in a world unto its own, with vast fields and unending countryside beyond.

Mac stepped out the front door, as if on cue, and met Ben halfway down the stone walkway, two mugs in hand. He offered one to Ben.

"So, what's this project about? You've got me curious." Ben blew on the steaming tea before venturing a sip.

"An anonymous donor has asked that we build a nativity scene. The vicar called me up early this morning to tell me."

"Nativity scene? I take it that means more than some little crate of a bed?"

"Aye, 'tis life-sized. Large enough to include a live Joseph and

Mary—a base, three sturdy walls, a roof, and a manger for the wee babe. We have a little over a week to completion, but we can finish the whole job in about four days' time. I'll be able to pitch in now and again, but I have other work to attend to…"

"And that's where I come in," Ben added.

"Aye. Come inside, and we'll talk specifics."

When Mac opened the dense wooden door to his cottage, Ben followed him inside, where the quaint space was dimly lit. The square footage was minimal—only a cozy sitting room to the right, a hint of the kitchen on the left, and a hallway probably leading back to a bedroom or two. Definitely a man's space, the home was filled with darker colors and no frills. A few paintings hung here and there, depicting hunting dogs or outdoor country scenes.

Mac led Ben straight to the kitchen and sat at a round table, where Ben joined him.

"We'll build this from scratch." Down to business, Mac took up his pencil and pointed to a thick pad on which he'd drawn an elaborate sketch. Even the shingles on top of the structure's roof were detailed. "We have no pattern," he explained, still pointing, "so we're on our own. I've determined the general measurements. We can mess about with the figures as we begin. Nothing set in stone yet."

"Mmm." Ben nodded as though he could possibly contribute anything at this stage.

"It's basically a three-step process," Mac continued. "There's lumber up at Mr. Elton's—leftovers from another project he had going. We'll have to haul it here to the cottage, where I've got the saws and tools we need. We'll cut the pieces to size then take 'em to the site outside the church for assembly. I'll arrange extra help for that part of the job. We'll need it."

"Sounds simple enough."

"Aye, in theory." Mac set down the pencil. "Let's get to it."

Ben was prepared to disguise his back and shoulder pain and dig in. He didn't want to give Mac any excuse to dismiss him.

Thankfully, though, today's heavy lifting of wooden planks into a van wasn't going to be just a two-man job. Mac had already recruited additional help. As they drove up to the farm in Mac's ancient, battered van, two other men stood near the farmhouse, chatting easily with Mr. Elton. Ben recognized Joe right away—his burly frame would surely shoulder much of the workload. The other man wasn't familiar. He looked younger, around thirty, maybe.

As they exited the van and approached the men, Joe waved at Ben while the other man extended his leather-gloved hand. "I'm Fletcher Hays. You're Ben, right? The Cartwrights' nephew?"

"Yes." Ben was getting better at filling the awkward pause before the lie.

"Great to meet you."

Ben recognized an American accent. "You're from the States. Southern?"

"Texas, born and raised. Not sure what the kids here will think of the accent. They might struggle with it."

"Kids?" Ben asked.

"Oh. Yeah, sorry. Students, I mean. I'm a new teacher. History."

Mac had given them time to get acquainted, but at this point, he seemed itchy to get down to business. He handed Ben a pair of work gloves, and the men took his cue and went to work. Ben's sore muscles had him cringing each time he stooped to grab the end of a new plank and chuck it into the van. But after half an hour, he grew numb to the pain. Or maybe the pain had worked itself out. They moved in silence, except for the occasional grunts and thuds of lumber into the van.

Joe had brought his van, too, so when the job was done, they made their way back to Mac's cottage, where the planks were unloaded. This process went faster, and before Ben knew it, the work was complete.

"Thank ye for your help," Mac told Joe and Fletcher. They all exchanged good-byes, and Mac said to Ben, "You're done for today, as well."

"Oh. I assumed we'd work into the afternoon."

"Alas, I'm committed to a couple of side jobs, so there's no time to show you how to cut the wood. But we'll start again Monday, early."

"Can we afford a weekend off?" Ben probably sounded overly eager, but he didn't care. He wouldn't know what to do with himself for forty-eight hours off. "I can work tomorrow, if you like."

"Nay, not necessary. We're on schedule for now. Can you put in full days next week?"

"Absolutely. I'm looking forward to learning a new craft."

"Aye, 'tis hard work but rewarding. Nothing like taking a shapeless piece of wood and building something grand with your hands. 'Tis my favorite kind of work, truth be told. Doesn't feel like work at all."

It struck Ben. "You've made those pieces in your cottage, haven't you?" He remembered the sitting room. "The rocking chair?"

"Aye."

"And even the kitchen table?"

"Aye." Mac chuckled, a hint of pink dabbing his cheeks as he kicked a pebble on the ground.

"Do you ever sell your pieces? You should start a business."

Mac shook his head. "Nay, 'tis only a hobby." He thought longer about it and shrugged. "I make carvings for my sister's grandson. For Christmas. Toy guns or a wee sailboat, that sort of thing." He steered the conversation sharply again. "About the nativity—you'll be paid at the end of the project," he noted.

"Oh. No, I don't need payment."

Mac stared with a confused frown, the crinkles in his forehead deepening. "Son, I can afford to pay ye."

"No, it's not that. I don't want people to know this, but"—he lowered his voice—"I don't really need the money. I'd rather work for other reasons. Let's just say I need this job. To keep me... occupied."

"Aye," Mac said as if he understood perfectly.

"Why don't you take what you would've paid me and donate it somewhere? A worthy cause."

"All right, son, if you're sure." The wrinkles had softened into acceptance. Possibly even respect.

"More than sure."

The walk back to Mistletoe Cottage felt restorative. Ben took the back route, behind the shops on Storey Road, to avoid meeting or talking to anyone. He reflected on Mac's type of work. In some ways, it was more rewarding than what he'd done for the past several years. There was something about working with your hands, touching the earth, the wood, being that close to nature. Working in silence with others and getting something accomplished together, something you could see take shape, right before your eyes. Something tangible. It might not be as important as saving a life, but it was still important, in its own way.

As he neared Mistletoe Cottage, Ben realized he'd been humming "The Messiah" in his head. He recalled the verse Mary had begun to read before the phone interrupted them: "a man of sorrows, familiar with suffering." He recalled that verse, somewhere in the back of his memory, but had never thought about it before—Jesus as a suffering man. As someone who experienced pain and loss, like any other human being.

And it struck him. Ben had always let the church, or his parents, decide who Jesus was for him—far away, hard to understand. Some vague shadow of a deity that rose so far above that He was never quite accessible. Ben had swallowed someone else's doctrine willingly all those years. But it was a vapid doctrine that came up empty when he needed it most. He couldn't find a single ounce of comfort in those clichés and trite rituals that everyone else seemed to bathe in without question.

But seeing Mary's faith this morning—the innocence of it, the unwavering confidence of her answers—certain questions had started to take root in his mind. Doubts about his own staunch, bitter beliefs about God. He didn't even know what those questions were, specifically. He only knew that a sweet older woman, holding a thick, antique Bible on her lap, had shown more passion for her God than anyone he'd ever seen.

Chapter Eight

External heat and cold had little influence on Scrooge. No warmth could warm, no wintry weather chill him. No wind that blew was bitterer than he, no falling snow was more intent upon its purpose.

~Charles Dickens

ROASTED NEW POTATOES, CHICKEN CASSEROLE, Caesar salad, French-cut green beans, roast beef, and more... how could she possibly choose? In the end, Mary decided not to. She shuffled along the makeshift buffet line, unashamed of dabbing small, measured portions of each selection onto her plate. After all, she had contributed two of the dishes—the miniature potpies and a quiche. That surely gave her the right to sample everything.

She had looked forward to the luncheon all week. Most people's eyes glazed over at the mention of committee meetings, but not Mary's. After-church meetings often involved generous potluck lunches and the chance to chat with women she didn't see through the week.

Making her way toward the long table in the church hall, she attempted to balance her overflowing plate without dropping a single bean or potato. Mary arrived at her spot and set down her feast. Amy Fitzsimmons, the Emporium owner's young wife, had already found her chair, across from Mary, and waved as she sat down.

"Amy, dear, you look wonderful. How's that precious baby of yours?" Mary asked, removing the napkin from the table.

"He's perfect," Amy said, flashing the grin of a proud mother. "He's such a good boy. Learned a new word yesterday. Doggie. Though he says it more like 'goggie' right now."

"So sweet," Mary said. She fought the vivid image of Sheldon at that age, sitting on his father's knee as he pointed out words in a book. "Apple. Bat. Car." When George started to close the book, Sheldon would grunt, frown, and point, until George opened it and read again. Sheldon's gleeful smile reappeared as George read for the hundredth time. Mary felt a painful ache inside her chest over the memory.

"Mary, this quiche is outstanding!" said Lizzie, Joe's wife, sitting two seats down. She pointed to her plate.

"Oh," Mary said, shocked back into the moment. Collecting herself, she added, "I'm glad you're enjoying it."

"You *must* give me the recipe. Joe would go mad for this. Maybe even add it to the pub menu." Lizzie dove in for another bite.

Holly approached the table and took a seat beside Mary, gently nudging her elbow. "Hi there."

"Hello, dear. What a pretty skirt."

"Oh, thanks." Holly brushed the green fabric with her fingers. "It's new."

Mary took a bite of casserole. "It was nice to see your sister in church this morning. Back from London already?"

Holly's seventeen-year-old sister, Rosalee, had recently embarked on a new career. Her role in a period piece for the BBC had been the talk of the village for weeks.

"Yes." Holly reached for her tea. "She returned yesterday. I think she was pleased with how her scenes came out. She's definitely found her calling."

"I'm so proud of her," a voice agreed. Mildred Newbury, Holly's new stepmother, was sitting catty-corner from Mary across the table. "And Bridget has found her way at last, I think. She's excited to apply for university. With her recent grades, I think she'll have her pick."

Mary was relieved that Bridget, Rosalee's twin, had straightened out. Over the summer, Mary had heard rumors of Bridget's slipping grades as well as a dalliance with an older boy.

Most of the ladies had found their seats and were chatting in between bites. The last to sit was the committee chairperson herself, Mrs. Pickering. She sat at the head, naturally.

"I didn't see your nephew. In church this morning, I mean," Mrs.

Pickering told Mary, loud enough for half the table of twenty women to hear.

Mary glanced up from her green beans and waved her fork casually. "Yes. Well. He was feeling under the weather. I insisted he stay at the cottage. No reason to have him spreading germs to the congregation."

"Quite right." Mrs. Pickering seemed to approve. "Very sensible."

After a half hour, giving the ladies time to finish their plates and exhaust all topics of conversation, Mrs. Pickering stood and rang a little bell to call everyone's attention. Then she lifted her notepad from the table, adjusted the glasses on her nose, and began the discussion of pertinent items regarding the Dickens Festival: the number of merchants participating with booths, seven this year; the Victorian costumes, which were coming along nicely; the program schedule for each of the festival nights; and the other last-minute issues to be decided.

The meeting was productive, but it lasted nearly three hours, in total, including the lunch portion. After sitting all that time, Mary found standing up without a wobble to be a challenge.

"Here, let me get this," Holly offered, nudging back the chair to give Mary more room.

"Thank you, dear. That helps. It was a quite a long one, this time," she muttered, out of earshot of Mrs. Pickering.

"She does have a tendency to ramble on," Holly concurred.

"Oh—I didn't see Noelle here this morning. I hope everything is all right with her pregnancy."

"Yes, as far as I know," Holly offered. "But she's so far along now that I think she tires easily. She wouldn't have lasted long at this meeting."

"Isn't that the truth?" Mary snickered.

Outside, waiting on a bench, George tapped his pipe against his palm and stood when Mary exited the church.

"When did you get out?" she asked, envious of him.

"A half hour ago." He supported her elbow, and they edged along the path toward Storey Road.

"And you've been sitting here, waiting on me all this time?" she asked.

"Well, Mr. Elton kept me company, up until about five minutes ago."

While Mary had attended her meeting, George was at rehearsal inside the church. He was playing Scrooge in the abbreviated version of the Dickens play presented during the festival. He'd learned nearly all his lines, but Mary knew she would have to quiz him in the next couple of weeks to make sure.

"How did rehearsal go?" she asked, stepping in synch with him.

"Oh, fine. No worries. A few minor bumps, but we'll get there."

She interlocked her arm with his and thought about how lovely it was to have a husband just the right height for her. He stood three inches taller—perfect for dancing. Not that they danced anymore. But if they were ever to dance, he was at a good height for it.

When they arrived at the cottage, Mary had hoped to hear piano music or perhaps to see Ben at the fireside, reading one of his spy books. Instead, the cottage was quiet, except for Bootsie's irritated mew, begging for a meal. From all appearances, Ben hadn't been out of his room all day, and it was nearing three o'clock. Mary wondered if he had taken ill. She contemplated knocking on his closed bedroom door to offer him food. But she reminded herself that he was a grown man, capable of living his own grown-up life.

After she and George had dinner later in the evening, she hemmed a costume while George snored softly in his chair. She heard Ben's door creak open. Instead of joining them in the sitting room, he ventured toward the loo then shut the door. Presumptuously, she put aside her hemming and went to warm up a plate. She'd made two pie tins of quiche that morning—one for the meeting and one for them, at the cottage.

Placing a generous slice into the microwave, she heard a door open. Ben shuffled into the room, his hair rumpled and a two-day growth of beard on his face.

"Hungry?" she asked just as the microwave beeped. She removed the quiche to set it down with a fork.

Ben only yawned, sat, and started to eat. Clearly, he didn't want to be disturbed.

She pretended to be busy in the kitchen and found some crockery to wash, giving him privacy without actually leaving the room. She'd only experienced less than a fortnight's worth of him, but based on observation, she knew parts of Ben quite well. But moments when he was closed off and inaccessible, in his own universe, made her wonder more about the parts she didn't know. *We've moved two steps backward again.*

The light and darkness of Ben was extreme. There seemed to be no middle ground or shades of gray. One day, she might get the inquisitive, polite Ben who offered to put away groceries, sit and watch telly with George, or even turn her dusty piano keys into a masterpiece. But the next day might bring gloomy Ben, the pensive, sullen man who grunted his answers and walked around her cottage like the shadow of a ghost, void of all hope. She wondered which one he truly was, deep inside. Surely, he hadn't always been both.

In the beginning, she'd been curious about that dark side of Ben. But after having seen the lighter side, she wanted more of that. She was interested in helping diminish the dark parts, helping to heal whatever wounds might have taken him there in the first place.

She remembered dark days, too. The hopelessness felt like looking up from the bottom of a deep, narrow well, into a light that was impossible to reach on her own. But, sooner or later, she'd had to make a choice: keep living that way and die a slow, painful death of the spirit or decide to live and to do more than simply exist. She'd chosen to get up, dust off, and move along, day by day. She hoped, soon, that Ben might choose that path, too. But she couldn't choose it for him.

Behind her, she heard Ben mutter his thanks and shuffle back to Sheldon's room. Mary cleared away his dish, put the quiche back where it belonged, and returned to her sewing, hoping the next day would bring him one day closer to crawling out of that well.

Chapter Nine

"I wish," Scrooge muttered, putting his hand in his pocket, and looking about him, after drying his eyes with his cuff: "but it's too late now."

"What is the matter?" asked the Spirit.

"Nothing," said Scrooge. "Nothing."

~Charles Dickens

"MAYBE THREE INCHES," BEN INSTRUCTED, tilting his head. "Or whatever you think. You're the expert."

Not that he cared whether his head was completely shaved. But he'd gotten tired lately of always tucking hair behind his ears, especially as he worked with Mac. So, when he'd paused at the window of Snippity-Do-Dah a half hour ago and caught a glimpse of his reflection in the glass, Ben decided it was time for a significant trim.

"Here?" the girl asked, taking a lock of hair between two fingers.

"Sure."

She seemed to be a rare hairdresser who preferred the quiet and didn't talk her customers' ears off just because she thought that was part of her job. Or maybe she, like Ben, was not a morning person. Either way, he was grateful for the silence.

Closing his eyes as she worked, he thought about yesterday—a bad day. His body was still being punished by hard labor that he wasn't used to, but the pain was more than that. It went deeper than muscular pain. He couldn't think of a single reason to get up and face the day. That familiar, suffocating cloud was back, and it hung over him, taunting him. He couldn't conjure up the strength to blow it away. So, he'd rolled over, shut his eyes, and begged his mind to fall asleep again. Easy way out—oblivion.

He recalled Mary's quiche and her concerned expression as she'd served it, probably wondering where the congenial Ben had gone. But he hadn't been able to summon the casual conversation it would have taken to reassure her he was fine. He wasn't fine. Why pretend?

The sudden, brassy hum of the blow dryer startled him, but the rush of warm air on his neck and his scalp made him close his eyes again. He wished he could return to this place in time, this peaceful warmth, whenever he sensed the darkness creeping in.

After clicking off the dryer, the young woman squeezed a circle of clear gel into her palm, rubbed her hands together, then massaged it into his scalp, sculpting and maneuvering the newly clipped hair the way she wanted it.

"All finished, sweetie." She unclasped the smock then removed it dramatically, like a magician's assistant waving her cape to reveal a rabbit's sudden disappearance. She popped her gum and admired her handiwork.

Ben glanced at the mirror and saw the old him reflected back—the clean-shaven, well-groomed man he used to be. Professional. Capable. Confident. Why wasn't transforming the inside as easily as transforming the outside? A few snips, a little gel, and *voila*!

"Thanks," he told her, counting out the pounds.

"Thank *you*." Her mouth widened into a generous smile.

For a second, he thought the smile might indicate more than gratitude—he sensed a bit of cheeky flirtation behind it. He didn't know what to do with that, so he dipped his head and walked toward the door with a quiet, "Bye."

Ben had exactly enough time for a quick stop before showing up at Mac's cottage. He walked past the Indian restaurant, then the Emporium, and found the bakery where he'd accompanied Mary last week.

As he entered, he saw an elderly man inside, to his right, sitting in a blue chair and wearing a friendly expression.

"Hello." Ben paused.

"Would you like a sample, young man?" He lifted his plate a few inches higher so Ben could see the bite-sized scones. His aging fingers trembled.

"Thank you." Ben chose a toothpick from the outer edge. "Mmm. Blueberry."

"My personal favorite," said the man.

"Mine, as well."

"You're a new face in town."

"Yes. Just visiting."

"I'm Alton Bentley."

"Pleased to meet you, Mr. Bentley. My name's Ben."

Another customer appeared behind him, eager to enter, so Ben left the sweet old man and made his way to the glass counter, which displayed rows and rows of sweets, pastries, breads, and cakes. He wondered how early the workers had to awaken in order to get them ready.

"Can I help you?" asked the woman behind the counter. She had sandy, shoulder-length hair and pretty dark eyes that looked hollow and tired. Perhaps she was the one who'd gotten up at an ungodly hour to put the treats in their places for people just like him.

"Err... sorry. I haven't yet had a chance to—"

"Take your time." She stepped back to shuffle through receipts as he struggled to make a decision. A minute later, he said, "I think I'll take the blueberry scones. Two, please."

She took a sheet of tissue paper from a box and reached in.

"The samples work, apparently," he said as she raised her head.

"Pardon?"

"I said, the samples work. The ones that old man is passing out." He pointed back behind him.

"That's my father."

"Oh."

"Yes, he loves being the center of attention. He's been doing that job for more than a decade. Usually, he sits outside, but it's too cold in December. He'll turn ninety this month."

"He doesn't look a day over seventy."

The woman chuckled quietly as she reached for a paper bag.

Before he walked off, Ben caught sight of something he hadn't noticed—chocolate croissants under glass. He hadn't tasted one since his honeymoon, nearly fourteen years ago.

Ben exited the bakery and turned toward Mac's place, but he couldn't stop thinking about those croissants—and his honeymoon. He let the memory have its way.

They'd been in Paris on their second day of holiday. Amanda had tugged at her new husband's sleeve and lured him inside a quaint café. She ordered two enormous chocolate croissants and two espressos then led Ben to a corner table. Amanda's smile was brighter than usual that day. She seemed blissful, happy in Paris, and happy with life. It was contagious.

As Ben sipped his espresso, Amanda tore her croissant and chattered on about Paris—the Louvre they'd seen that morning, the outdoor cafés, even the size of their glamorous hotel loo. She told him she wanted to return to Paris for a future anniversary.

Ben watched his wife. Her words evaporated while he cued in on her familiar mannerisms—the way her thin, feminine hands danced along with her dialogue, the way she swatted at that one loose strand of sandy-blond hair that always dangled near her cheek, and the way her eyes widened when she punctuated certain words. He loved to watch her tell stories, even if they sometimes had a tendency to ramble on.

And in that moment, watching her flick the flakes of croissant off her fingers, Ben felt a powerful surge of love for her. Beyond the lavish wedding, the expensive honeymoon he'd saved up for five months to pay for, beyond the hoopla of parties, and beyond rituals and toasts to the happy couple, everything amounted to just them. The two of them had started a life together. Partners. Friends. Companions.

Their life together had only just begun to unfold. There, in the little café.

"Ben? Did you hear me?" Amanda had tilted her head and blinked at him.

"Every word," he lied. Then he reached for her hand and stood, raising her delicately from her chair as her confused smile widened. And then he kissed her, slowly and deeply, right there in front of a roomful of strangers. He barely heard the "oohs" and a smattering of applause around them. When he backed away, he saw tears in his wife's eyes.

"I love you," she said.

And that was all he ever needed to know.

By the time Ben reached Mac's property, he had forced away the blissful honeymoon memory. All he would *ever* have left of Amanda were memories. And so, that momentary bliss always turned to torture.

Mac, without knowing it, had the perfect antidote waiting for Ben—the precision of carpentry. Ben could turn off his emotions for a while and use the logical, rational side of his brain. The moment Mac began to speak in mathematical terms, Ben understood. He'd had no idea how precise carpentry needed to be. But it was right up his alley—designs and measurements and figures. His field of study had prepared him for such things, in a sense.

They sat at Mac's kitchen table for an hour, going over the sketches for the nativity scene again. The plans were even more detailed than they'd been before. Mac had worked hard over the weekend. He patiently explained to Ben all the steps involved—the measuring, cutting, and anchoring processes. He pointed to the designs with the pencil's eraser as he spoke. Finally, during the assembly near the church, a sturdy base would be attached to the side walls, along with a back wall and a wood-shingled roof. Then they would add an angel up top—one that Noelle Spencer had painted for last year's Christmas play. The project was far beyond what Ben had expected, in terms of scale and detail.

"Think you can handle it?" Mac asked then chewed off the end of the scone.

"I do," Ben said. He didn't know if Mac really believed him—or whether he even believed himself—but he would spend the rest of the day proving it to both of them.

Mac gathered up the papers he'd spread all over the table. "Let's get started, then."

They spent the next two hours in Mac's work area behind his cottage. He'd converted a small cabin structure into a substantial toolshed, fit with a couple of benches, three saws, and an entire wall of tools hanging on hooks.

The first thing Mac did was hand Ben a pair of safety goggles and gloves, then he showed Ben how to use the different saws and how to mark the proper measurements. Ben got the hang of it almost immediately, and soon, he was doing the cuts on his own while Mac supervised.

"Guess I can leave you to it, then," Mac said as Ben cut his fourth piece of wood without any guidance. "I've got a few stops to make this afternoon. There's always something to do around the village."

"I can imagine," Ben said. "You're in high demand."

"Aye. 'Tis rare when I get a day off."

Mac started to leave, but Ben stopped him. "Mac, I should tell you something."

Mac paused, his face wearing the same matter-of-fact expression it always did.

"Well..." Ben removed his goggles. "You should know the truth. I'm not their nephew. Mr. and Mrs. Cartwright, I mean. We're not related."

"Aye," Mac said, his face unchanging.

"You knew?"

"Suspected."

"I think I should explain..."

"Nay. None of my business. If the Cartwrights feel close enough to call you their nephew, that's good enough for me," he said with a firm nod then walked toward the open door.

If he'd revealed the truth to anyone else in the village, Ben would've had to call up the Cartwrights and let them know their cover had been blown. But Ben knew in his own gut that Mac would never say a word.

Secure in that knowledge, Ben replaced his safety glasses, switched on the old radio nearby to a seventies rock station, and moved on to the next piece of wood.

"Your *hair*!" was the first thing Mary said when Ben entered the cottage several hours later.

He'd forgotten all about it. He rubbed at the back of his head, touching the bristles of newly shorn hair with his fingertips. "Just a little trim." He shrugged.

"I like it," she said, getting a closer look. "The cut reminds me of my Sheldon's. He used to wear his hair that length. And he used to put... jelly? Or mouse..."

"Mousse?" Ben corrected with a grin.

"Yes, that's it. Mousse. Messy, foamy gunk. But it made his hair look so handsome..."

He watched her eyes go distant and cloudy.

"What's for dinner?" George asked loudly, clapping his hands as he entered the room.

Mary blinked and forced a smile. "I don't know. What are you going to make for us, husband?" She winked up at Ben and faced George, who gave her a quick peck on the lips.

"I don't think you'd enjoy burnt steak or rubber chicken, my dear."

"George." She swatted his arm. "You know I was teasing. I thought we'd do breakfast for dinner. How does that sound, Ben?"

"Uhm... fine," he said, his mind still on Mary's faraway look. Ben had assumed that Sheldon was somewhere in another city, busy raising a family. But Mary's look told him that perhaps Sheldon was *too* busy. Come to think of it, Ben hadn't witnessed any communication between Sheldon and his parents—no letters or phone calls—and Mary hadn't mentioned his coming to visit for Christmas or that he might reclaim his bedroom. Something didn't feel right...

Soon, Ben sat down with George and Mary to a filling dinner of eggs, sausage, toast, and jam. Ben talked freely about the nativity, about all his newly acquired carpentry skills, and about how much progress he had made.

"I can't wait to see it," Mary said. "I think Fletcher and Holly are signed up to be Mary and Joseph, at least for two of those nights."

"Why didn't they ask *us*?" George said, straight-faced, sopping up his egg with the last bit of toast.

"Is that a serious question?" Mary paused to look at him. "We are *much* too old." She looked at Ben with a half grin. "Can you imagine, the two of us as Mary and Joseph?"

"Well, you've got the name right," Ben played along.

"You two. Stop teasing." She stood up to clear her plate and took George's, too, as he swiped the last sausage from it.

"It's so easy to do," said George. "You make it irresistible." He scooted his chair from the table and joined her in the kitchen. "We'll take care of this, love. Why don't you go and sit down. Rest your feet."

"Well, if you're sure." She wiped her hands on a dishtowel.

"We're sure. Aren't we, Ben?"

"Positive."

"All right, then." She rubbed her forehead with her fingertips. "I think I'll go have a proper lie down. I seem to have the beginnings of a headache."

She padded through the sitting area and down the hallway.

Two hours later, when she still hadn't emerged from the bedroom, Ben assumed that she'd decided to retire for the evening. In the nearly two weeks he'd stayed at Mistletoe Cottage, Ben hadn't seen Mary go to sleep before midnight.

Since he'd slept away the previous day, Ben was anything but drowsy. So instead of turning in after dinner, as he usually would have, he decided to join George by the fire. Ben stretched out on the sofa, his feet hanging over the edge, a Tom Clancy book propped on his abdomen. George took his place in the recliner across from him, reading something called *The Shack*.

After a while, George snorted then stirred in his chair. He closed his book, removed his glasses, and stretched his arms above his head with a grunt.

Ben shut his book, too, to see if George was heading off to bed. When George's arm came back down to his lap, Ben noticed the picture frame behind him. He'd seen it before but not with his fresh questions about Sheldon. "Can I ask something?"

"Of course." George suppressed another yawn and leaned back, intertwining his fingers.

"About that picture behind you…"

George arched his neck to see. In the picture, Sheldon stood a foot taller than both his parents, encircling their shoulders with his arms as they stood in front of a Christmas tree. All three smiled widely for the camera. "Oh, yes. Sheldon and the two of us. Just before his final term at university."

Ben shifted to a sitting position, elbows on knees, to get a closer look.

George grabbed the frame and brought it closer, his eyes filling with memory. He handed the picture to Ben, who examined it while George spoke. "It was a fine day. Sheldon's last day of exams. He was going to be an architect—"

"'Was'? What happened to him?" Ben handed the frame back.

When George locked eyes with Ben, his pupils turned the color of burnt orange, reflecting the dancing fire off to the side. Ben regretted the question immediately, and he wished he could snatch it away and put it into his pocket for another day. Not once in the previous two weeks had either George or Mary pried into his personal life, despite having every right to do so. Still, there he was, asking a deeply personal question he had absolutely no business asking.

"I'm so sorry, George." Ben shook his head. "I truly didn't mean to—"

"It's fine." George gazed at the picture and sighed a long, thoughtful, burdened-down sort of sigh. "It happened the very night this photo was snapped. Sheldon had come home for the Christmas holiday and was eager to spend an evening out in London with some childhood mates from the village—good lads, all of them. But Sheldon hesitated because he thought it was bad manners, leaving us on his first night home. But Mary insisted. She wouldn't spoil his fun, and she reassured him we'd all have plenty of time to spend together. When the lads picked him up here at the cottage, Sheldon asked for a photo beside the tree—he and his mum had decorated it when he first arrived—then off he went with the lads, to celebrate the end of term." George wiped his eyes. "Mary got the call an hour later." His voice broke under the weight of the words. "The lads didn't even make it to London. There had been an accident on the way." His bottom lip quivered as he barely got the words out. "A drunk driver had sideswiped their car. The other two boys had minor injuries. But our Sheldon... he was killed instantly."

Ben felt the sharp pull in his abdomen, where his ulcer still lingered. The pull shifted to nausea as a wave of anger came. A young person's life being snuffed out too soon—it confirmed to Ben the unfairness that existed in the world. The pain in George's eyes was too familiar, and for his own selfish sake, Ben wished he'd never asked the question in the first place. It was too hard, walking down that excruciating path again, even with someone else at his side who knew that shared pain.

"I'm so sorry," Ben whispered, his eyes downcast. "For your loss. And for bringing this up. I didn't mean to bring back the memory for you."

"No. It's all right." George wiped his cheeks with one hand then leaned back to replace the frame. "It's not a memory that ever leaves me for very long. I remember it every day, in some form. But it's *good* to remember. Not the loss, but who he was. What he meant to us."

"What was he like?" Ben sensed that George wanted to tell him.

"A carbon copy of Mary. In personality, at least," George mused. "Positive-minded, amiable. Chatty. He could be mates with anybody. That was his greatest gift, I think."

Ben nodded. "That's definitely a gift, trusting people enough to create a friendship."

"And, of course, we have no idea where the height came from. Six foot two, he was. My great uncle was tall, and so was a distant relative on Mary's side. You know, I've always thought that tall men, in particular, have a harder time being humble."

"What do you mean?" Ben asked.

"Well, just that they see the world from such a greater height than the rest of us. They look down on people, whether they mean to or not. Can't help it. And I think, for some folk, that sort of goes to their heads. But not Sheldon. He was the most humble soul I've ever known. A gentle giant, we called him. Would give the clothes right off his back to help someone. He gets that from Mary, too." He corrected himself. "*Got* that from Mary."

"I can see that," Ben agreed. "She saved my life."

"Do you know, that was my first thought, after we found you in the snow? I thought to myself, 'Sheldon would be so proud of his mum right now.' Isn't it odd? After all this time—thirteen years, nearly fourteen now—and he's still my first thought."

Ben fought the prick of tears as he wondered whether Amanda would still be his first thought, even decades later.

"Well." George slapped his knees. "I suppose I'd better go join the missus in the Land of Nod." He grunted to stand. "Good night, young man. May you sleep well."

He patted Ben on the shoulder as he passed by.

"You, as well," Ben said.

Hearing the bedroom door close a minute later, Ben moved his gaze to the fire. He wondered whether he would ever be able to think about Amanda with that kind of acceptance or that sort of closure and peace. George hadn't shown a trace of wrath against the drunk driver who'd stolen his son's life—only sadness at his loss and gratefulness at having had Sheldon as long as they had.

But picturing Amanda's beautiful face in vivid detail, Ben didn't think that kind of acceptance would ever come for him. All he could feel when he thought of her, if he ever felt anything at all, was regret.

Chapter Ten

Darkness is cheap, and Scrooge liked it.

~ Charles Dickens

MARY SHIFTED TO HER SIDE and stared at the rose curtains. Thirty-five years old, they were the same ones she'd had since first moving in to Mistletoe Cottage. She studied the pattern of vines, daintily entangled up the fabric. Mary had slept well enough, but she'd awoken to a gentle ache she hadn't experienced in a very long time. She didn't want to do anything but stare at curtains. George must have sensed it and known she needed to be alone with her thoughts, so he snuck off to work early after making his own breakfast and gently kissing her forehead.

Her thoughts wandered back to Ben and to the question that had become more prominent each day since he'd arrived.

Why?

Why had this person been placed quite literally on their doorstep? Was his presence in their lives some sort of sign? The coincidences were too strong to ignore—the height, like Sheldon's, the obvious intelligence, like Sheldon's, and the new haircut, like Sheldon's. He even occupied Sheldon's virtually untouched room.

Why?

What was she supposed to gain from Ben's visit? At first, she'd thought it was nothing more than an opportunity to show kindness to a lonely man, especially during a holiday season. But the longer he stayed, the more she became convinced his purpose went deeper than that. Deeper than a few bowls of soup or a stack of laundered clothes.

Perhaps they were supposed to learn something from each other in the bigger scheme of things. But what?

She shifted in the bed and stared at the ceiling, thinking about Sheldon. He was always there, every day, tucked into the corner of her mind and her heart. But she rarely allowed herself to walk fully back to that corner and face him with her eyes wide open. It took great effort, after so many years, to paint the details of his smiling face, the light dusting of freckles on his cheeks, and the exact shade of blue in his eyes. Time had faded the details and dulled the edges until they were blurry. And it was easier not to conjure them at all.

But sometimes, she had no choice. Sometimes, he seemed to beckon her.

Mary closed her eyes and saw him—ten years old, cross-legged at the fireplace, cocoa in hand, discarded wrapping paper strewn around him. That particular Christmas, everything had gone horribly wrong. George had twisted his ankle in the snow and been ordered to ice and elevate it the rest of the day. Mary had baked the most beautiful mince pies and promptly dropped all but one on the kitchen floor. Only minutes later, Pronto, the family cat, had decided Christmas Eve was the perfect time to become fascinated with the tree, which had toppled suddenly, breaking three antique family ornaments. After picking up the jagged pieces and discarding them like ordinary, everyday rubbish, Mary had locked herself in the loo and sobbed into a hanging towel.

But when she emerged minutes later, Sheldon had salvaged the remaining mince pie and divided it into three small slices. He handed Mary hers with a loving smile.

"Mum, don't cry. We can share."

Mary fought tears again and sniffed. "Thank you, my darling." Sheldon folded into her arms as she gripped the plate tightly, careful not to let it drop. She kissed the top of his head as she looked across the room at George—foot hiked up on two pillows, eating the last bite of his share. Pronto's eyes glowed from behind the sofa.

"Mm. Delicious, Mary." George winked as he set down his plate.

Sheldon led Mary to the sofa, where he'd already set out their gifts. The tradition was to open presents on Christmas Eve and save the stockings for Christmas morning.

"You go on," she said. "I'll watch you while I eat."

He got to work, ripping open the shiny gold paper to reveal a train set. His face said it all. "Mum, Dad! How did you know? I've wanted one for *ages*!"

It was Mary's turn to wink at George as she polished off her last bite. She didn't have to open a single present to know she was blessed. She didn't have to have perfect mince pies or ornaments intact. In the end, those were merely things. And watching Sheldon's eyes sparkle beside the fire as he admired his new toy, she had all the Christmas she needed.

Years later, Sheldon had referred to that evening as his "Best Christmas Ever." And she couldn't help but agree.

Feeling tears dampen her cheeks, Mary wondered what he would've become, had he avoided the drunk driver by five seconds, or even two. *Bizarre, how swiftly a life is taken. In only a blink.* Sheldon would've been a successful architect and maybe found a beautiful wife with long blond hair. He would have had three children—two boys and a girl, who also had blond hair. And he would have visited every Christmas and brought along her grandchildren. He would have made the holiday what it should have been—pure joy.

Since the accident, Mary and George had learned to make Christmas special, all by themselves, attempting to recreate those special times. Each year, she made George put up the outside lights and find the perfect Christmas tree, while she put out the gingerbread figures on the mantel and laced festive ivy along the window frames. It was what Sheldon would have wanted. But underneath the external trappings was a void that couldn't be filled by lights, tinsel, and Bing Crosby. She knew it, and George knew it. But they could never say it aloud.

But, for the first time in years, she had someone else to look after at Christmastime. In fact, until that morning, she'd spent very little time silently fighting that whisper of Christmas depression that came along each year. Ben's arrival had taken her focus off herself.

"Enough," she finally said to the air, pulling back the sheets and swiveling her stiff body to put her feet on the cold floor.

She couldn't waste the day thinking about things she couldn't change. Besides, she had a rehearsal to get to. Life had a way of moving forward, whether she wanted it to or not.

After waking at dawn, Ben took a long bath then put the kettle on. Rather than stay indoors with it, he took his tea to the back garden. On his way out, he passed George, who was off to work earlier than usual. Because neither of them were "morning people," they just mumbled their good mornings.

A bird singing a very specific tune had led Ben outside. He'd first heard it while stirring his tea. Unlike most people, he tended to think singing birds were rather annoying—all he heard were random notes and even irritating repetitive pitches. But the unusual bird that had caught his attention seemed musically trained. The whistle was beautiful, even rhythmic. Twittering staccato notes were filled with resonance and tone, building to a full-length bird symphony, from beginning to end.

By the sound of it, the bird had likely perched somewhere in the back garden. And opening the door, Ben spotted it immediately—a splash of orange against the bleakness of a bare winter tree. He closed the door quietly, careful not to spill his tea, and studied the bird. It lifted its brown head high, opened its beak, and repeated the song, just for Ben.

"Beautiful, isn't it?" Mary had quietly opened the door and stepped out with him.

"Yes." Ben held the door for her as she came through. "It is."

"I call him Henry." She folded her arms for warmth.

"Why Henry?"

"I don't know, exactly. He looks like a Henry."

Ben took another sip. "So, he makes regular visits, does he?"

"I first saw him about two weeks ago. He's come and perched on that very branch nearly every day since. Usually this early in the morning."

"I hadn't heard it before now," Ben said. "Or, rather, hadn't paid attention."

As though understanding their observations and becoming suddenly shy about having an audience, the bird jumped high and disappeared into the sky, leaving the black pencil-thin branch to quiver in his absence.

"You're up early," Mary noted, turning to look up at Ben.

"You, too."

"I guess it's because I went to bed so early last night."

"Sleep well?"

"Quite well. Thank you." She placed her hands into the pockets of her dressing gown and said, "I'm very proud of you."

"Proud?" He wrinkled his brow, wondering what she could possibly mean. He hadn't even checked George's list yet. In fact, he hadn't accomplished anything except to have a bath.

"Because you haven't run away yet. Even though I know you desperately wanted to."

Ben shrugged. "Well, you and Mr. Cart—George—have made it easy to stay."

"You're safe with us here, you know." Her gaze was unwavering. "Whatever it is that you've run away from, it won't find you here."

Ben shook his head. "I wish that were true. But it's in here." He pointed to his chest. "How do you run away from yourself?"

"If I knew the answer to that, I'd be a rich woman, wouldn't I?"

"Indeed." Ben polished off his tea in one gulp.

"Well, I'm freezing my bum off." Mary chuckled. "Let's go inside. You have a nativity to build, and I have another rehearsal to attend, then a shift at the bookshop. Must keep busy, mustn't we?"

Rachel, the vicar's wife, tapped her wand on the music stand and poised her hands. "Ladies, let's start at measure sixteen. Sopranos, you're carrying the melody, so I need your voices loud and strong during this section."

Mrs. O'Grady played the jangly piano as the ladies sang, "Ding Dong Merrily on High..." The song was one of Mary's favorite Christmas tunes. Her mother had sung it to her when Mary was a little girl.

"Beautiful!" Rachel exclaimed when the song came to an end. "I think that will be one of the highlights. Well done, ladies. Let's take a little intermission. Say, ten minutes?"

Immediately, everyone began talking with the person next to them, picking up where they'd left off an hour before, when they'd first arrived. The rehearsals were equal parts musical and social, and Mary could never decide which of the two she enjoyed more.

Only a couple of the ladies took their break offstage. The rest stayed where they were but spread apart, in order to have more room to converse, which usually involved hand gestures.

"Are you nearing the end of the countdown?" Mary asked, turning to Noelle, the only one sitting down in a chair.

Noelle put a hand on her protruding belly. "Twenty-one more days."

"Doesn't that final month seem like three combined?" Mary sympathized.

"It really does. Every muscle aches. Every movement takes extra effort. But little Adam will be worth all of it."

"Adam! So you've decided on the name."

"Finally. Adam didn't want to name his son after himself—it would make the fourth Adam in his family. But I couldn't think of any other name I loved more than my husband's."

"That's precious," Mary said, and she meant it. Noelle and Adam's love story was one that the village had seen unfold shortly after Noelle came over from America. The childhood sweethearts had reconnected after years apart. The best kind of love story.

Noelle turned to find her bottled water, leaving Mary to overhear someone else's conversation. The twins, Holly's teenaged sisters, stood giggling together. They were nearly university age, and over the years, especially the past year, Mary had watched them mature and grow into beautiful young women.

"I stood behind him at the bakery yesterday," Bridget said. "He's *so* tall. He's a giant!"

"A *handsome* giant," added Rosalee. "I saw him this morning, walking on the other side of Storey Road. I like him without the beard. But he doesn't smile very much, does he? Looks a bit... intense."

"But that makes him all the more mysterious. He broods. Like Mr. Darcy."

"Ooh, yes! Our own Mr. Darcy in Chilton Crosse!"

Mary could hardly contain her chuckles as she eavesdropped, knowing precisely whom the girls were admiring. She could just picture her "nephew's" cheeks flushing red at the mention of it.

"Ladies." Rachel tapped her wand, drawing everyone's attention gradually forward. "Time to start gathering again."

After setting the shingle perfectly in line with the rest of the row, Ben used the staple gun to secure it in place. He'd completed a fourth of the roof for the nativity when he heard Mac's footsteps shuffle on the dusty floor of the shed.

"Impressive." Mac stopped in front of the workbench and crossed his arms to assess Ben's work.

Removing his goggles, Ben looked up. "Thanks. Made good progress this morning."

"I see. Looks professional. I don't think I could've done better myself."

Ben rubbed his fingertips together. The pads of his fingers had grown raw over the course of the afternoon spent handling wood. But adding shingles was a tedious process that required a careful touch. He'd quickly learned that work gloves only got in the way. And besides, the extra effort was worth it. He had to admit, it did look professional. He'd been so concentrated on setting one shingle at a time that until that moment, he hadn't stepped back to see it as a whole.

"We're right on schedule," Mac confirmed. "We'll haul everything to the church in the morning for assembly. An all-day job."

"Looking forward to it. It'll be good to see this thing put together."

"Aye. Should be a sight."

Ben rubbed his neck, sore from stooping over the shingles with intense concentration. "This village certainly knows how to 'do' Christmas. A live nativity, the Dickens Festival. And I hear there's a sleigh ride, as well?"

"Aye. Mr. Elton's mare. She's hearty but gentle. This may be her last year to pull the sleigh, though. Getting old, like the rest of us."

"Mary told me something about a Mystery Claus? A Father Christmas who goes about the village, dropping presents on people's doorsteps. And he's been able to conceal his identity all these years?" Ben watched Mac's eyes for a change in expression or a flicker of admission. But he saw nothing of the sort.

"Aye. Everyone wonders who 'tis."

"Who's your guess? Any suspicions?"

Mac scratched his silver-stubbled chin and pondered his answer.

"My money's on Duncan Newbury. Richest man in town, with a heart of gold."

"Hmm. Interesting. Haven't met him yet."

"A good soul. My mate for many years."

"Well, whoever the Mystery Claus is, I applaud him. At least he gives people something tangible to believe in." Ben picked off a dab of glue that had stuck to his palm.

"Tangible, as opposed to..."

"I guess, as opposed to *just* faith. I mean, this mystery person—he helps people. He gives them something physical, meets their actual needs instead of offering prayers that won't go anywhere." He caught Mac's tilt of the head and wondered if he'd offended him. "Look, I'm not knocking people who have faith. I admire those who believe in something they can't even see. But in my profession, I was taught to be logical, to make assessments and judgments based on facts. I just... well, I have a hard time believing in things I can't see with my own eyes." He wiped his hands together, dusting off the dried glue.

"Your profession?" Mac raised an eyebrow.

Ben realized the hints he'd given. He could either lie or be frank. *Time to make a quick decision.*

"I'm a physician," he admitted. "Well, *was* a physician. Until about six weeks ago."

"Aye?" Mac raised the other eyebrow, showing genuine surprise.

"A heart surgeon." Even uttering the words felt strange. He hadn't thought of himself in that way for so long. In fact, the more he'd been separated from it, the more blurred his identity had become. He tried to connect his thoughts back to his original point. "So, because of that, I've been trained to deal with issues in terms of symptoms, test results, procedures—things I can see, things I can do something about."

Mac nodded, but the hesitancy in the nod told Ben he didn't agree. The nod was more of an "I'm listening" courtesy nod. Although Mac was never vocal about it, he might well have been a religious man with a silent faith and a very private relationship with God. Ben hoped he hadn't crossed any invisible lines or moved down a peg or two in Mac's eyes.

"I believe that people have a right to believe whatever they wish to believe," Mac said, his voice steady.

His worry evaporating, Ben smiled his agreement. But Mac wasn't finished.

"Still, faith in a higher power can be an anchor for some people. Especially those in danger of drowning."

Before Ben could process what Mac could've meant, a dog barking in the distance startled him. A man walked up the hill with a Border collie at his heels, dancing around him, heralding his arrival.

"Hey, y'all," said Fletcher, approaching the doorway. "Thought I'd see if you needed a hand on that nativity. Are we puttin' her together?"

"Nay, not today." Mac bent down to rub the dog's ears. "In the morning. Could use your help, though, loading the van."

"Sure. No problem. Oh, there was something I wanted to ask you..."

Ben could tell he wasn't needed in the conversation, so he quietly stepped back to focus on the shingles. As reached for his goggles, he tried his best to swat away the image of a drowning man—and the idea that he might be the very person Mac had in mind.

Chapter Eleven

There was a frosty rime upon the trees, which, in the faint light of the clouded moon, hung upon the smaller branches like dead garlands. Withered leaves crackled and snapped beneath his feet.

~ Charles Dickens

THE SMALL TROUGH LOOKED RUDIMENTARY and rickety, as it should have, with splintered wood and rustic dimensions. Ben had arrived early at Mac's shed to finish constructing the manger. Studying his accomplishment, Ben was satisfied with the end result. When Mac returned from another job, he, Ben, and Fletcher loaded the manger, along with the pieces for the entire structure, into vans and drove them to the church. The task of assembly required non-stop lifting, balancing, hammering, gluing, and more lifting. And still, they hadn't yet added the roof.

Ben was ready for a substantive break when Mac asked, "Are you up for more manual labor? Another project starts day after tomorrow." Mac probably should've waited to ask the question for a moment when Ben *wasn't* pouring sweat, stretching his agonizing back muscles, and wondering what he was about to get himself into.

For some reason, Ben let his mouth answer before he could think about it. "Okay. What is it?"

"The festival. We've got the booths pre-made and jointed, but they need to be set out, with some minor repairs made. It's a two-day job, several hands on deck. Interested?"

Ben took a long swig of bottled water then wiped his mouth with the back of his hand. He'd stripped off his jacket thirty minutes ago, even in the nippy forty-five-degree weather. When he stopped moving, he felt a sudden chill.

Reaching for his jacket, he said, "Sure. Count me in."

Though his tortured body was on the verge of crying out, "No!" Ben knew deep down that he couldn't miss being part of the festival. He enjoyed contributing and being behind the scenes of something bigger than himself. And, certainly, in some small way, he was giving back to a village that had already shown him kindness. Besides, he didn't have anything else to do with his days.

"Okay, where do you want her?" a voice said from behind.

Ben turned around to see an angel, a full meter tall, wobbling toward them. The man lugging it had dark, wavy hair and wore a trench coat.

"'Tis lovely, indeed," Mac said, studying it as the man set the angel down. "Noelle did a beautiful job." The fiberglass angel had an ethereal face, but her warm expression was almost human.

"Thanks. I agree. But I'm sort of biased. Noelle was nervous—hadn't painted on anything but a flat canvas before. She worked hard on this. Do you think it can be secured well enough on the roof?" The man peered up at the structure.

"Aye, no problem," Mac said.

The stranger noticed Ben then steadied the angel with one hand while reaching out his other. "Hi. Adam Spencer."

"Ben Granger. Nice meeting you." He shook Adam's hand.

"Mary's nephew, right? The one from London?" Adam asked.

"Ben's my new apprentice," Mac added with a satisfied nod. "Hard worker."

Fletcher had been hammering away in the background while they talked, and he approached them, out of breath. "Hey, Adam. How goes it?"

"Everything's good. Keeping busy."

"Must be," Fletcher continued. "Haven't seen you around lately."

"Yeah, I've spent a lot of time back and forth to London, trying to get some things in place before the baby arrives. I want to take a bit of time off when that happens. We'll see."

"Oh," Ben said as the lightbulb came on. "Spencer. I think I met your wife—does she own the art gallery?"

"That she does," Adam said. "Inherited it from her aunt Joy."

"Not Joy Valentine... the Cotswold artist."

"That's the one."

Ben grinned and shifted his weight. "You won't believe this, but I actually purchased one of her works at Sotheby's, at that auction. Three years ago, was it?"

"Almost exactly," Adam confirmed, looking impressed. "Noelle found those paintings in a locked room of her aunt's cottage after she died. That's where we live now, Primrose Cottage. Just up the hill." He pointed south.

"The piece I purchased is from a series called 'Freedom,'" Ben said. "It's this seagull, hanging in mid-air above the ocean. She captured it so well. I think her work is brilliant."

"Thank you. I'll tell Noelle you said so. She'd love actually knowing someone who bought the painting. Where is it now? Did you hang it in your flat?"

He'd asked a perfectly reasonable question, but Ben didn't have a reasonable answer. Ben had gotten so caught up in the conversation about the painting that he'd almost let the wall crumble entirely. But he erected it again as he remembered his situation. "Err... yes. Yes, my flat."

The truth was, he didn't know exactly *where* it was. He'd left his London townhouse in such a fog on that evening six weeks ago, physical objects hadn't mattered, not even his mobile phone. Material things had all lost their importance long before that night when he'd packed a quick bag. He'd had no idea of his destination, only that he'd needed to leave, to escape the pain. Suddenly, he wished he'd been careful enough to salvage a few things. Maybe Martin had saved the important items for him and put them in storage somewhere, on the off chance that Ben would return someday. That night, Ben had written his best mate a text, a suicide note of sorts, only he hadn't intended to kill himself. No need. He already felt dead inside.

"Well, it's nice to meet a fellow alien. I mean, Londoner," Adam joked. "Seriously, Chilton Crosse welcomed me with open arms. And there's nothing like a Christmas spent here. Quite an experience."

"Speaking of..." Mac prompted. "Are you here to help out or just deliver this beauty?"

Mac reached for the angel, tipping her toward him.

Adam removed his trench coat and started to roll up the sleeves of his expensive-looking shirt. "Put me to work!"

In the remaining hours it took to finish the nativity structure, Ben couldn't stop feeling shaky. Partly, his body was weak from the physical exertion. But he'd also been caught off guard by the talk of London and the painting. It was jarring to picture that townhouse again, a place he'd spent so much of his time with Amanda. Then on top of it, seeing Noelle's life-sized angel had reminded him of another angel—the one he carried with him, always.

Fortunately, the group had completed the nativity project without conversation. Ben wasn't in the mood for more talk. Each man had worked together in relative silence, except for the occasional suggestion to move, tighten, or level something.

"Good work," Mac said as they stood back to get the full picture—a life-sized structure, large enough to fit life-sized people. Ben had to admit, it appeared solid, sturdy, and well constructed. He would never have believed a few days ago that the wood he'd cut would amount to a work of art. All four of the men had taken nearly an hour to secure the angel up top, but it was the crowning jewel.

"Lagers at Joe's, everyone. On the house." Mac slapped Ben's back.

"Sorry. I need to be somewhere else," Ben mumbled, hoping Mac would understand. "Thanks for the offer, though."

Ben would've enjoyed the camaraderie of celebrating a job well done. But he was grumpy and edgy—not exactly the recipe for good company. He needed some place to sit and stew, where he could be alone. The last thing he wanted to do was be jam-packed into a booth at a rowdy pub, hearing happy people trade humorous stories and laugh at each other's jokes—people living a carefree life.

As he zipped his jacket and watched the other men head toward the pub, Ben wasn't sure *what* he wanted to do. Retire early? Read the last of his spy novel? Eat a meal he wasn't hungry for? Nothing felt right.

For the first time all day, he stared up at the sky, really studied it. The orange hung at the edge of the horizon. Fanning out in front were spectacular red, yellow, and purple clouds. *Rainbow clouds*, Amanda used to call them. In fact, if he hadn't been shivering under his jacket and if the air hadn't been so crisp and cold that it stung his lungs, he would have sworn it was a summer sunset. Such a Technicolor palette seemed out of place in a winter sky.

Hands in his pockets, he let his legs take him where they wanted to go. He wasn't ready to go back to Mistletoe Cottage. Earlier, he'd noticed a road leading off to the side of the church that he hadn't yet explored. His legs took him in that direction. He walked briskly at first, his breaths puffing out in a rhythmic beat. But when the road became steep and hilly, his instinct wasn't to stop and turn back. It was to tackle it head-on. Running up the incline was almost easier than walking up it—something to do with the speed and momentum. He removed his hands from his pockets and ran. And ran.

He ran for at least a half mile, until his legs went numb and his lungs felt the stabbing pain of freezing air. Slowing his pace, he noticed the faint tree-lined path to a spectacular mansion that glittered with dazzling lights and had Christmas trees out front. A sign up ahead told him it was Chatsworth Manor. *This village is full of surprises.*

He could hear the cheery voices of people gathering at the entrance. It looked like a party—one he didn't wish to join. So he reversed his path and within minutes, stomped his way back down the hill at an easier pace. Seeing the dim glow of church lights ahead, he moved closer. The building was probably empty, offering just the sort of solitude he was looking for.

He entered the church and was relieved to find that it was, indeed, empty. Walking the main aisle down the center, he kept his eyes on the stained glass forming a cross behind the pulpit. The symbol of faith was a comfort for so many around the world. He almost wished it could comfort him, too.

To the left of the pulpit, in the corner, stood a magnificent old piano. He couldn't resist. Just as his legs had taken him up the hill, his fingers drew him to the keyboard.

He sat down, lifted the lid, and placed nimble fingers on the ivory keys. He played one note, then two, then three. A few notes later, he was playing Beethoven's Sonata No. 8. His favorite piece, it had invited a standing ovation at his last concert, eons ago. The music came in a rush. Though he'd rarely played as an adult, his fingers still held the memory of the notes. The crescendos and diminuendos. The staccatos and the shifting tempo. He remembered all of it vividly. Hearing the music echo in that small space, bouncing off the stone floor and filling the room with magic, Ben's state of mind was marginally better. Some of the angst exited through his fingers, and the keyboard absorbed it.

Finished, he lifted his hands and let the final notes linger. He wondered why life couldn't always hold the kind of beauty those notes produced, why the beauty couldn't last instead of having to end. Why did there have to be so many minor cords, such dissonance?

When Ben reached the door of Mistletoe Cottage, he panicked. It was gone. Reaching into his jeans pocket, he couldn't feel that familiar cold silver or the blunt edge of the angel's wings. He wondered if he might've dropped it during the afternoon, with all that moving, stooping, and bending. Or maybe he'd lost it during his impetuous run up the hill.

He inserted the key Mary had given him two days before. Peeking inside, he saw only Bootsie, who was curled up and snoring softly on the end of the sofa. He recalled that Mary and George were out to dinner at the Newburys'. Being the "nephew," he had been invited along but had declined.

He shut the door and walked past the cat, into the corridor, and into Sheldon's room. He couldn't recall where he'd last seen the angel, though he always kept it on his person, tucked safely inside a pocket or sometimes in his wallet. He felt again, to make sure he hadn't been mistaken. He searched his bag first. Then he unzipped pockets, shoved his fingers deep into their crevices, and finally tipped the contents of the bag onto the floor. He rummaged through it, frantic, hoping to see a flash of silver.

He couldn't lose it. The angel was the only thing of value he possessed.

Panting, he threw down the empty bag in frustration and rocked back on his ankles. Rubbing his thighs with his palms, he racked his brain.

"Where *is* it?" he grunted through clenched teeth.

He decided to return to the worksite of the nativity. He would scour the cold, damp ground all night, if that was what it took. But then he thought of the jeans he'd worn the previous day, the ones he'd slung over the chair. Mary hadn't laundered them yet. He reached for them and dug his long fingers into one pocket. He came up empty and began to lose hope again. But when he thrust his hand into the other pocket, he touched the comforting cold silver, gripping the grooves of wings and the folds of a dress. *My angel.*

Clutching it, he sat back on the bed and ran his fingers through his hair. Losing the angel would have been like losing them both all over again.

He opened his hand and tilted his palm toward the bedside lamp. He thought about the day he'd bought the angel for Amanda and remembered the surprise in her bright eyes. She'd clutched the angel to her chest and leaned in to kiss him. He could still recall the exact pitch and lilt of her voice as she half-squealed into his ear, "I *love* it!"

The pendant had been more than an angel to them. It represented years and years of hormone shots, fertility treatments, doctor visits, disappointing news, and—finally!—success. All that time, they had never lost hope. They'd been counseled on the emotional dangers of trying to have a baby under such grueling, uncertain circumstances. Fertility treatments sometimes did enough damage to split couples apart. But unlike most couples, Ben and Amanda bonded over the shared desire for a baby.

So, when the pregnancy test came back positive, they'd held their breath, having been through the scenario before. And weeks later, when the sonogram told them they were having a healthy little girl, hope rose again. *Maybe this time...*

And when the pregnancy progressed so far that Amanda was confident enough to suggest a name, Ben went straight to Tiffany's and pointed at a representation of that name under glass. Angelina. Angel. Their angel.

He remembered that hopeful moment and compared it to his current despair—the empty vacuum his life had become. And Ben started to weep. The torment rose from the bottom of his abdomen, up to his face, then rushed out in painful dry heaves.

He was back inside the nightmare—a harrowing dream where he was being chased, and no matter how hard he ran or how loudly he yelled, he was merely running in place, all his cries silenced. He was trapped, with the monster catching up to him. Always catching up to him.

Ben's breathing slowed as the heaves calmed themselves. He wiped his face with harsh strokes, angry about having entered that hollow cavern. *Utterly pointless.* Tears never brought anyone back or made the burdens easier to bear. He hadn't allowed himself to weep, not even at the funeral, as his mother-in-law placed a comforting hand on his back while the casket was lowered into the ground. Ben had felt so cold and numb that day. When the shock wore off weeks later, the pain had truly begun...

He stood and tucked the angel down inside his jeans pocket then kneeled to place the scattered items back into his bag—an effort to turn chaos back into order. *As if that's even possible.*

Chapter Twelve

Christmas was close at hand... it was the season of hospitality, merriment, and open-heartedness.

~ Charles Dickens

BEN LISTENED AT THE DOOR to be sure. There it was again—the muffled yell that had awakened him two minutes before. He cracked the door to hear George spouting nonsense in the other room, punching important words: "I will live in the *Past*, the *Present*, and the *Future!* The Spirits of *all three* shall strive within *me!*"

Ben shut the door, reached for his jeans, and pulled them on with a yawn. Mac had given him the day off. Ben and the others had worked tirelessly over the weekend to assemble the festival booths, seven in all, along the edges of Storey Road. Four of the booths had required minimal work. Because their walls were already connected with strong hinges, assembly had been a snap. But three of the booths had been used for many years over and had needed significant repairs. But the work was finished in time to give the vendors a couple of days to set up for the festivities.

Spying the clock on the dresser, Ben was surprised he'd slept so late—10:36. He usually woke at the crack of dawn.

He nudged open the bedroom door, deciding his growling stomach couldn't wait. Creeping into the sitting room, he tried not to disturb George, who faced the window, his hand raised in the air. But George must've sensed someone and turned around with a start.

"Sorry," Ben said.

George laughed his husky laugh. "I didn't think anyone was here."

"Mac gave us the day off," Ben explained.

"Ah."

George extended a rolled-up script in explanation. "I'm taking the morning off to rehearse. I must've sounded barmy, standing here all alone, yelling like a lunatic."

Ben shook his head and stepped closer. "Not barmy—diligent. Sounds like you've got the lines down pretty well."

"Can't quite get this one page memorized." George pointed to the opened script. "I've considered scribbling some dialogue on my arms. As a reference. But don't tell Mary."

"No, of course."

"Think you could run some lines with me? I could do with the practice. Mary always interrupts and tells me how to 'punctuate' certain words. I can never do a full run-through with her."

Ignoring his hunger, Ben caved. "Certainly. Be glad to."

George found the right place in the script and handed it over to Ben. "Okay. I'll start with 'Step this way.' Middle of the page."

"Got it." Ben held his finger on the line.

"Step this way, if you please," said George as Scrooge, using a hand gesture for emphasis.

Ben as Bob Cratchit cleared his throat and said his lines: "It's only once a year, sir." The script asked him to "plead," so he added a whine to his tone. "It shall not be repeated. I was making rather merry yesterday, sir."

They rehearsed the scene twice, as George faltered on a couple of lines, then they moved on to another scene. Then another. An hour and a half later, they'd been through the script once through, and Ben handed it back to George, who smacked it against his open palm with confidence.

"Excellent!" he said. "This has made all the difference. I think I've got it now. Might not even need to cheat, after all. Let me buy you a pub lunch to thank you, eh?"

"Only if I'm the one who pays. And I won't take no for an answer, so don't even try."

"All right, then. If that's the way it has to be." George grinned. "I'm famished!"

Four lagers and two shepherd's pies later, Ben and George reclined in their comfy chairs by the pub's fire, their appetites filled to the brim. They'd used up most of their language for the script run-through, so little was said during lunch. Ben didn't mind. He enjoyed George's company partly because he never felt the pressure to fill the gaps in conversation. And when they did talk, it was usually about rugby scores or favorite novels.

Taking another swig, Ben noticed someone approaching the table: a woman in her sixties, wearing a long blue coat and a matching blue hat.

"Hello," she said to Ben, extending her hand. He took it out of politeness and shook it gently, wondering if he should have known who she was. She looked a little familiar. "I've heard so much about you." She offered a star-struck smile.

"Oh?"

"You're the nephew. Ben Granger," she told him.

"And you are?"

"Elda Pickering." She finally let go of his hand but continued to smile.

"Nice to meet you." The name finally registered, and Ben realized precisely who the woman was. Mary had told him all about Mrs. Pickering, the village gossip—snooping, unrelenting, and incorrigible. He wasn't in the mood to dodge questions, so he fumbled for a way out.

"How long do you intend..." she started.

Beyond her, Ben saw his salvation—Joe lugging in a silver keg through the front door. Seizing the opportunity to escape, Ben began to rise as he told Mrs. Pickering, "Awfully sorry—Joe needs my help... nice meeting you." He walked briskly past her and toward the bar.

"Could you use a hand?" he muttered as Joe set the keg down.

"Well, sure. But you're eating, aren't you?"

"Trust me, you'll be doing *me* the favor." He pointed discreetly toward the table.

Joe saw Mrs. Pickering. "Ahh..."

Ben followed him outside to the van, where the last two kegs sat, and reached for one of them.

"You wouldn't be interested in helping, would you?" Joe asked, hoisting a keg with a soft grunt. "Setting up the booth tomorrow then working during the festival? That's what these are for." He waited until they'd lugged the kegs inside and set them down. "We're serving a bit of ale and some wassail. You know, the Dickens theme and all."

Ben stretched his back and thought about it. He hadn't even

considered what he would do once the festival began. Since all the booths had been constructed, he supposed he was out of a job.

"Sure. Count me in." Working with Joe would give Ben a way to stay on the fringes of the festival, where he could observe things from the sidelines rather than participate fully, as he might have been expected to do.

"Great," Joe said. "If you can be here early, around seven, we can get started with the preparations."

"Right. Anything else I can do right now? I've got all day, if you could use me."

"Those are dangerous words, my friend. I can always think of something."

George approached the bar and whispered to Ben, "Smart thinking, your escape. She got the hint, looks like." Mrs. Pickering had moved on to chat with someone at the next table.

"Oh. I hadn't meant to leave you there alone."

"No bother. I'm used to her." George approached Joe. "Can I get a shepherd's pie to go? It's for the missus."

"And it's on me." Ben reached for his wallet.

George opened his mouth in protest.

"Remember our deal?"

"That didn't cover Mary, too."

"Sure, it did, Uncle." He slapped the pound notes on the bar.

"Comin' right up." Joe took the money and disappeared into the back room.

The darkness was an element of winter that Mary could easily have done without. She stepped out of the Book Shoppe at four thirty to a muted-gray sky, no trace of sun. She didn't enjoy the messy, drizzly, bleak weather they'd been having the past few days. Her lovely Christmas snow had disappeared. And long winter nights tended to make her sluggish and sleepy, especially after busy days when she had lengthy rehearsal, a luncheon, then an extra shift at a busy bookshop. She was eager to get home and rest. As she walked toward Mistletoe Cottage, her feet throbbed.

She glanced to her right, at all the booths along Storey Road, each covered with enormous green tarps, making them look like alien pods that had landed during the day. Earlier, on her walk, she'd seen people hard at work decorating their booths with signs and Christmas décor. Mary hoped she would feel more like celebrating once the festivities commenced. Right at that moment, however, all she felt was overly tired and even a bit cranky.

Bah. Humbug.

Inside the cottage, she found George on the sofa, snoring. On his chest, rising and falling, was the script. She tried not to wake him, but Bootsie's meows startled him, and he jumped, grabbing the script before it fell to the floor.

"I'm sorry, love." Mary closed the door.

George rubbed his eyes with his knuckles. "No, it's fine. I can't believe I fell asleep. I hadn't intended on it."

Mary removed her gloves and scarf then approached the sofa. "Why not? You work hard. You deserve a good nap."

He tugged her hand and brought her over to sit with him then pulled her closer, squeezing her shoulders with a comforting hug. She snuggled up inside his strong embrace.

"You've had a long day," he said. She could hear his voice resonate inside his chest.

"Too long," she agreed. "I'm knackered." Her eyes were drawn to the blazing fire. "Mmm, this is lovely." Her eyelids began to droop under their own weight.

"You want your coat off?" he whispered.

"I'm still cold. I think I'll keep it on for now. It's positively bleak out there, George. Gray skies, drizzly weather. It makes me melancholy."

"I know," he said, and she wondered if he really did know.

"How was your day?" she asked, eyes still closed.

"Fine. Good. Spent the morning with Ben, actually. We had lunch at the pub."

"Did you?"

"He stayed there, helping out Joe with some things. I suspect he'll be here soon. I brought home some pie for you. Shall I get it now?"

"No, I want to sit right here with you, just like this. The pie can wait." She nuzzled up closer, her face near his neck. They hadn't cuddled for ages.

"About Ben..." George started. "I've meant to tell you something. A conversation we had a few days back."

"Mmm..." she said to let him know she was listening.

"It was about Sheldon."

She opened her eyes as though it would help her listen more accurately.

"Ben had noticed the picture of the three of us from that night. And he asked me about it. And I didn't see any reason to lie, to cover things up."

"No," she agreed. "No, of course not."

"So, I told him everything. About the boys' trip to London, the accident..."

Mary remained quiet, uncertain how to respond.

George continued. "Ben was very kind about it. He seemed genuinely interested—and empathetic. I think it surprised him, that we'd lost a son."

Mary shifted her body enough to look up at him without removing herself from his grasp. "Do you think that..."

"What?"

"Well, that Ben has experienced... a tragedy of his own? Ever since he's arrived, I've seen this hollow look in his eyes—a sadness I recognize."

"Yes." George gazed into the fire. "I've seen it, too. But I've also seen some hope. There seem to be moments, unguarded, when the sadness goes away."

"But they don't last very long, those moments. I think he's fighting it. George, do you think he'll ever confide in us? About his loss?"

"I don't know, dear. I hope so. A man shouldn't carry that kind of burden alone."

She laid her head back down on his chest. "George?"

"Yes, my love?"

"I'm glad we have each other."

"I am, too."

He kissed the top of her head, and her eyelids grew heavy again. This time, she let them have their way.

Chapter Thirteen

But every man among them hummed a Christmas tune, or had a Christmas thought, or spoke below his breath to his companion of some bygone Christmas Day, with homeward hopes belonging to it.

~ Charles Dickens

I T DIDN'T MATTER HOW OLD she got or how many years passed her by. Mary still had occasional flashbacks of childhood moments at unexpected times. And when they came, they were as vivid as the day she'd lived them.

Opening the December 21 door on the wooden advent calendar, Mary recalled her mother's anticipation as she waited for little Mary to peek into a door each day and discover the treat inside—a trinket, a chocolate, or a special note from Father Christmas. Mary could still see the creases of her mother's fingers and smell the lavender scent of her perfume as she leaned over and helped Mary unwrap the treat. *Simple days. Glorious days.*

Looking back always filled Mary with an equal measure of bitter and sweet. She enjoyed having had those days in the first place but was sad they were gone forever. Her mother, her father, and even her brother were long gone...

The soft chime of the mantel clock told Mary she was late.

"Blast," she whispered, turning from the calendar to search for her coat. Since the morning when she'd allowed herself to lie in bed and wallow in memories of Sheldon, she had been off-kilter. Even the gift wrapping and cookie baking she'd done the night before as a necessary distraction weren't distracting enough. She couldn't seem to snap out of it. The more she tried to jump back into that cheery Christmas mood she so desperately craved, the harder it became.

In fact, wrapping her scarf about her neck, Mary thought of how she was cheating herself. More than any other day of the year, one day had come to be her favorite—the first day of the festival. The whole village would be coming together to kick off the celebration. She always anticipated the music, costumes, food, games, and sleigh rides. Any other year, she would've been the first one outside, helping the vendors or browsing the booths, out of sheer eagerness to see it all begin. She loved to watch the children's smiling faces and see Mr. Bentley dressed as Father Christmas outside the bakery, passing out Christmas sweets. *But not this year, not today.* She would rather stay snug in her cottage than participate.

Still, Mrs. Pickering would come knocking at her door if she remained absent for too long, so she buttoned the final button, patted Bootsie on his sweet little head, and stepped out of Mistletoe Cottage, wishing that at least the weather would have cooperated. At least a dusting of snow might have made it easier for her to pretend. But she peered upward to see a bright-blue sky and damp patches on the ground after last night's rain.

Breathing in, Mary shut the door and found her happy face, reminded of the one Eleanor Rigby kept in a jar by the door. Mary had always thought that was what the Beatles' lyric meant—the "social" face people put on before stepping outside, in order to blend in with everyone else. As she produced a smile, Mary could feel the corners of her mouth turn up and the hint of wrinkles form at the corners of her eyes. Having George at her side would have helped. But the festival began on a weekday this year—no time off for the postman during the busiest season. Still, he would be changing into his Scrooge costume each night to wander about the village, staying in character with all the other Dickens characters. Now *that*, she couldn't wait to see.

As she neared the first booth, Mary heard a melody drifting from the other end of the street—classical, Victorian, and Dickens-sounding. Joe's wife, Lizzie, was in charge of the music, and Joe had helped set up the sound system the previous night. Mary and the festival committee thought it a good idea to have music playing in the daylight hours, as people shopped. At night, there would be live music—a children's concert, madrigals, and even a harpist. Of course, the grand finale, a Christmas Eve concert, would include the ladies' choir. She only hoped they were prepared enough.

"Mary!"

Hearing her name, she crooked her neck to see Joe, across the street, waving at her. Outside the pub was a booth decorated with a sign: Ye Olde English Pub. Underneath it, assorted sweets, treats, and drinks filled the shelves of the booth.

When Mary crossed over to meet him, Ben appeared with a friendly "May I interest you in some roasted chestnuts?" He held out a paper bag, stuffed full.

"Oh, they smell delicious." She reached for her bag.

"No, no." Ben waved her money away. "For you? On the house."

Mary thanked him and took the bag. "The booth looks wonderful. Have you been stocking it all morning?"

Ben nodded and suppressed a yawn. "No rest for the weary, eh?"

People had started to gather, and Mary was suddenly in the way. "I'll be going," she told Ben. "See you later on!"

She nearly ran into a little boy in Dickens-wear, presumably Tiny Tim. To her right, she saw Mr. Bentley, wearing his hood and rich-red costume. He sat in his usual chair outside the bakery.

"Why, good morning, Father Christmas," Mary said, approaching him.

"Hello, young lady." Mr. Bentley reached to find his plate of samples. "Care for a gingerbread?" His voice sounded gravelly with age.

"They look marvelous." She took the smallest one. "Thank you."

Children had started to gather behind her, to see Father Christmas and to sample his treats. She backed away to give them room and decided to see if Holly needed any help. She and Amy Fitzsimmons were sharing a booth this year—Holly displayed coffee-table books and gift items, while Amy offered small antique reproductions, toys, and lace from her Emporium.

"Mary!" Holly waved as she approached. "Wonderful to see you. Isn't this fun?"

She was wearing a colorful holiday sweater, with miniature candy canes as earrings.

"It is!" Mary replied. "I'm here to offer my services. Is there anything I can do?"

Holly chewed at her lip. "If you want, you can be in charge of taking the money." She showed Mary the cashbox and calculator then unfolded a chair for her. "Will this be okay?"

"Certainly," Mary said, grateful for a way to participate in the festival today without actually participating. She could remain behind the scenes, out of the way.

Last week, Ben had spotted the ideal gift for George while passing by a shop window, but he hadn't had time to purchase it. After working non-stop at the pub booth on the first morning of the festival, he finally had time. Around noon, Joe insisted Ben enjoy the rest of the day, peruse the booths, and mingle with the villagers. Instead, Ben walked along the pavement behind the booths, where there was less traffic. All the shops were still open, minimally staffed, so Ben headed straight to Smoke & Mirrors, a small tobacco place sandwiched between the bookshop and a dress shop. Established 1743, the sign read.

As he walked inside, Ben noticed immediately the claustrophobic atmosphere—long walls created narrow halls packed with items on every shelf, ceiling-high: cigars, pipes, tobacco, backgammon games, flasks, and pocket knives. Classical music was playing, and the dark wood tones and hunter greens of the walls reminded Ben of an exclusive men's club. The stench hit him next—that acute, pungent odor of dozens of tobacco brands all mingling together into one spicy scent. His sinuses stung as he inhaled, and he wondered how the shop owner, Mr. Belvedere, kept from passing out every time he turned the key in the lock. Surely his senses were dulled to it.

"May I help you?" Mr. Belvedere asked, folding his newspaper. He sat at the back of the shop, behind a glossy wooden counter. He had one of those bristly moustaches that reminded Ben of a thick and wiry horse-grooming brush.

"I'm looking for a Christmas gift," Ben replied. "A pipe. Your very best." Ben knew that George smoked an occasional pipe—Mary either approved of or simply turned a blind eye toward the habit.

"I know just the one," Mr. Belvedere said. A stout man with a beer-barrel chest, he had trouble climbing down from his high stool. When he finally teeter-tottered his landing, he paused and looked up at Ben, squinting and pointing. "Aren't you..."

"The Cartwrights' nephew," Ben acknowledged. "Yes. Yes, that's me. The pipe's a present for George."

"Yes. Well, follow me." Mr. Belvedere walked the length of the shop until he reached the pipes. He touched three boxes before tapping one on the upper shelf and announcing decidedly, "This is the one."

He uncapped the box with great reverence, as though revealing a precious diamond. Though Ben had no expertise with pipes, when he saw the smooth, grainy wood and slightly arched neck of the pipe, he could tell it was a quality piece.

"Beautiful finish, a fine choice," Mr. Belvedere said, playing the eager salesman. "One hundred ten pounds."

"I'll take it."

Following Mr. Belvedere to the register, Ben knew that George wouldn't have minded the cheapest pipe in the shop. He wasn't the fancy type. But Ben *wanted* to get the best. He had so few opportunities to show him gratitude.

Minutes later, Ben walked past the toy shop. He hadn't planned to enter—he had no need to buy anything for a child. But, seeing a basket filled with wooden toy sailboats, he paused then stepped inside.

As he waited for the teenaged sales girl to approach, he reached for one of the sailboats. "Do you know who makes these?"

"He's a local. Mr. MacDonald," she confirmed. "He brought those by yesterday, and we've already sold three."

"Make that four." He reached for his wallet. He would keep the boat for himself or maybe give it to a random child as a gift. The purchase was a nice way to make a small, anonymous donation toward his friend's hobby.

Remembering his mission, he pressed on. Finding Mary's present hadn't been half as easy as finding George's had been. It took scouring and hunting—things Ben had little patience for. But when he did find it, at the Emporium across the street, it was the one. Within minutes, the saleswoman had wrapped the gift and placed it into his hands. He could hardly wait to see Mary's face.

After leaving the shop, he crossed the street and spotted a pair of jet-black Mickey Mouse ears bobbing inside the crowd—little Bobby, who had been through so much in his young life. Without thinking, Ben stepped in front of the boy's parents with a sincere smile.

"Excuse me. I'm Ben Granger, nephew of Mary and George Cartwright."

A flash of recognition crossed the woman's face. "Yes, nice to meet you."

"Well, I have something for your little boy. I don't have any use for it, and I was looking for someone who might." Ben reached inside one of his many bags and produced the wooden toy sailboat. A wide grin spread across Bobby's face.

"For me?" he asked.

"Just for you," Ben said. "If it's all right with your parents, of course."

The mother nodded, patting Bobby's shoulders. "Say thank you to the nice gentleman."

"Thank *you*!"

"Happy Christmas," Ben added before they parted ways.

He started to head toward Mistletoe Cottage again but noticed activity near the church. The nativity scene had attracted a gathering. He took a few steps in that direction to get a better view and saw Fletcher and Holly, dressed in their Biblical attire, arranging themselves inside the structure. Mrs. Pickering fussed over them, smoothing out Mary's costume and fidgeting with Joseph's fake beard. Ben felt a bit of pride as he saw it all come together, knowing he'd played a quiet role.

Hoping to be the only one at Mistletoe Cottage so that he could place his gifts beneath the tree incognito, Ben clicked his key inside the lock and pushed open the door. Mary sat in her rocker, needlepointing. She noticed Ben and removed her glasses. Bootsie meowed, at her feet.

"Well, hello," she said. "I expected you well after dark, with all that activity at the pub."

Ben shut the door, set his packages nonchalantly on the sofa, and took a seat nearest Mary. "Lizzie took over for me. I'll go back this evening and see if they need another hand."

"Did you enjoy yourself?" She eyed the packages then replaced her glasses and returned to her project. "At the festival?"

"Well, the booths were too crowded for me, actually. So I did a bit of browsing in the shops, instead. I didn't expect to see you here, either. Figured you'd be working at a booth or maybe rehearsing."

"There's a rehearsal later this afternoon. The final one. I hope we're ready."

"You will be," Ben reassured her.

He rubbed his hands together, feeling the heat from the fire. Having a gap in conversation with Mary was unusual. Even when he didn't want to talk, she always seemed to find something to fill the space so easily. But there she sat, rocking, focused on her needlepoint.

He recognized the stoic look on her face. Others might interpret her expression as concentration as she watched the needle go in and out. But this was different—a sadness behind the eyes.

Helpless to fill the gap on his own, Ben reached inside his bag for the wrapped package, the size of a hefty encyclopedia, and held it in front of her. "I have a present for you."

She removed her glasses again and stared at the shiny gold paper. "For me?" Her eyes grew wide.

"An early Christmas present. You can have it now."

"Right now?"

"Yes." He chuckled. "Right now."

She set her needlepoint on the ottoman and accepted the package. "What have I done to deserve this?" She looked like a little girl with bright eyes, excited to be told she had a surprise.

"Everything. I wanted to do something special. Besides, it's nearly Christmas, isn't it? Close enough, at least."

"I suppose it is." She found a crease in the paper and dug her fingernails in to unwrap one end. "What have you done here?" she asked, her smile turning to a sly grin. He could see her trying to work out in her head what the present might be.

Ben couldn't remember the last time he'd felt such eager anticipation, waiting for someone's reaction. This was the "better to give" part of that old platitude. He would much rather watch someone else open one of his presents than open one of his own.

Mary neatly folded the gold wrapping and set it aside. Wriggling her fingers inside the gap of the brown box, she popped the tape. "My, this is elaborate," she whispered. "Did you wrap this?"

"I'm not nearly that talented."

Lifting the flaps and peeking inside, she touched the tissue paper and reached in, digging deeper, until her hands found something. She looked up at Ben then raised the something out of the box. He leaned in to pull the box down and away from her, so she could see the gift fully. She set it into her lap and stared intently at the mahogany box, topped with miniature skaters on an oval-shaped patch of ice. A Christmas tree stood at the end of the scene, with snow all around.

"It's musical." Ben reached over to twist the gold knob. It started to play.

"'Ding Dong Merrily on High,'" she acknowledged, humming along. The skaters glided along the ice, drifting to the tinkling music. "It's so beautiful." She met his gaze with surprise in her eyes. "Thank you, Ben. How incredibly kind of you."

"You're the one who's been kind to me. This is the least I could do. I wish I could do more. There's no way to repay you for what you and your husband have done."

Mary shook her head but didn't speak. Tears had filled her eyes, and suddenly, Ben felt responsible. "Oh, no. I didn't mean to make you cry." He reached for the tissue box on the other side of the sofa and offered it to her.

"Ignore me. I'm a silly woman." She dabbed at her eyes with a tissue. "I don't know why I'm crying. But it's such a lovely gift..."

"Well, I'm thrilled you like it. I saw it in the shop and knew it already belonged to you."

He could tell she was forcing more tears away. Then she lifted the music box out to him. The skaters were slowing down as the song dwindled. "Here. Would you find a place for it, please? On the piano, I think."

"Certainly." He took it from her and found an empty spot that seemed the right fit.

"You knew exactly how to cheer me up," she said as Ben returned to his seat. Then she laughed—a hearty chuckle he hadn't heard from her before.

"What is it?" he asked.

She smoothed out the tissue in her hands. "Well, here I am, bawling my eyes out like a baby, telling you I'm all 'cheered up.' I'm a funny old thing, aren't I?"

"I think you're a lovely thing." He reached over for her free hand and clutched it.

She squeezed it back. "Ben, would you do something for me?"

"Name it."

"Would you consider… staying? I mean, past the holidays? I don't think I could bear to have you leave us so soon. You've become part of the family, in a way. It would make me so sad to see you go."

A sting of tears hit Ben unexpectedly. He hadn't thought past the end of today, much less the end of the holiday. Surely, he'd imposed on them long enough. But as he thought about it, a part of him couldn't imagine how hard it would be to leave Mistletoe Cottage, either. Not yet.

He cleared his throat. "I'll consider it. No promises, though. Okay?"

"That's good enough for me."

Chapter Fourteen

He was conscious of a thousand odours floating in the air, each one connected with a thousand thoughts, and hopes, and joys, and cares long, long, forgotten!

~Charles Dickens

BEN HAD ASSUMED, QUITE MISTAKENLY, that the second day of the festival would somehow be less frenzied and less crowded than the day before had been. But the morning produced double the crowd of the previous day. Perhaps they were tourists who'd heard about the Dickens Festival from their tour guides. Or maybe they were people who'd wanted to avoid the first-day crowds. Whatever the case, Ben stayed at the pub's booth all morning, helping to serve the masses.

When Ben took his lunch break, he finally stretched his aching back, took his leave from the madness, and tried to feel human again. On Ben's way out, Joe had thrust a Styrofoam box into his hands, and Ben knew immediately it was the shepherd's pie he'd been craving for the past hour. He couldn't wait to devour it.

Working his way around the village toward Mistletoe Cottage, he spotted Mac, bent behind one of the booths, struggling with something.

"Need a hand?" Ben asked.

Mac grunted and straightened up to face him. He pointed at the booth with his screwdriver. "Bollocks hinge," he muttered. "They can't use this shelf until it's fixed."

"Can I have a go at it?" Ben handed Mac the shepherd's pie and bent down on his knees to get a better look. After struggling a couple of times to fit the hinge back on, he knew it was futile. "Seems beyond repair," he said.

"Aye. I have another that size, back at the shed."

"I'll fetch it," Ben offered.

Mac hesitated then agreed. "Sure you don't mind?"

"Not a bit. I need the exercise. I've been standing at that same post all day. I'd love a jog up the hill. Stretch my legs…"

Mac produced his keys and gave them to Ben. "The hinges are in the second drawer of the workstation. Near the back wall."

"Back in a jiff."

"What about this?" Mac asked, holding up the Styrofoam.

"Have you eaten?"

"Nay."

"It's yours. Compliments of Joe."

Ben took off before Mac could protest, weaving his way through the crowd, choosing the quickest route to Mac's cottage.

Minutes later, he stood in the shed, rummaging carefully through drawers. He didn't see the hinge in the second drawer, where Mac had suggested it would be. He didn't find it in the other drawers nearby, either.

He surveyed the entire room, scouring it for another possible spot. He noticed a second workstation tucked into the far corner of the shed. Ben reached for the only drawer, a wide one, and dug through packs of screws, extra nails, some odds and ends—and saw a hint of brass. The hinge was identical to the broken one.

Before Ben closed the drawer, a pair of black mouse ears caught his eye. He peered closer. The ears belonged to a large, thick white envelope. "Your Walt Disney World Vacation Package" was printed in colorful, bold letters on the front. The package likely contained everything— expensive day passes, hotel reservations, possibly even plane tickets. And he could picture the smile on Bobby's face when he saw those mouse ears on Christmas morning.

Mary's words from weeks ago echoed in Ben's mind. *Our mysterious Father Christmas leaves things on doorsteps. He gives people exactly what they need.*

"Indeed, he does," Ben said aloud, his voice bouncing off the slate floor.

He flipped the envelope over and laid it in the drawer, back where the information belonged, safe and sound—and anonymous, just as Mac had meant for it to be.

Mary hummed along to the Christmas carol piped in from Joe's sound system as she walked the paper cups of wassail to Holly's booth. Somewhere between last night and the second morning of the festival, Mary had begun to feel infinitely better about Christmas, about the festival—about life. She felt more like her old self. And rather than question why, she decided simply to enjoy it.

And the recent temperature drop, combined with the hint of gray clouds, gave her the slightest hope that they might have a bit of Christmas snow, after all.

As she turned the corner of Holly's booth, Mary heard Fletcher's voice.

"When?" he asked into a mobile phone.

Mary joined the small crowd of women—Mrs. Pickering, Holly, and Lizzie—watching his face intently. She wondered what was wrong.

"Mm-hmm," Fletcher said. "Is she okay?"

Mary knew something was wrong. She set the cups down on the change table and waited for an explanation.

"Yes." He nodded. "Sure, I'll tell them. What about later tonight? Eight o'clock? Sounds good."

"Well?" Holly said with frustration as he tapped his mobile off.

"That was Adam. Noelle had her baby a couple of hours ago."

A chorus of "Oh!" went up all around.

"But... isn't it early?" Mary did the math in her head. "Two weeks early, at least?"

"I think so," Fletcher said, "but the baby's perfectly fine. Adam says he thinks the due date was about a week off, anyway."

"So, spill the details—when did it happen?" Holly asked.

Fletcher grinned his cowboy grin and tucked his hand into his jeans pocket, clearly enjoying being the only source of information for all the eager ladies. "Adam didn't say much—only that she started having contractions early this morning at the cottage. So he rushed her to the hospital in Bath, and she had the baby about thirty minutes ago. He says she might be up to visitors later tonight. If all goes well, she'll bring the baby home tomorrow."

"I can't believe how quickly they rush women out of the hospital these days," Mary chided. "Back in my day, they let us stay at least three days, sometimes even a week!"

"I want to go see her," Holly said, turning to Mary. "Will you come, too?"

"Count me in!"

"What about the nativity?" Fletcher said.

"Oh." Holly paused. "I'll see if Bridget and Riley will take our places. They'd make an adorable Mary and Joseph, wouldn't they? They could be our understudies." She pulled out her mobile and tapped the number.

Mary saw "Scrooge" approach the booth, wearing his top hat and frock coat she'd hemmed last week, and when he came to stand beside her, she clutched her husband's jacket sleeve. "Dear, did you hear the good news? Noelle has had her baby. Little Adam."

"That's marvelous. Everyone healthy?"

"Yes, thankfully. I was worried because he was a bit premature. Adam says we can go and visit her tonight. In Bath."

"Who's going?" George wondered.

"Probably just us girls," Mary said. "Though the men are certainly welcome to join us."

"I'll go." Fletcher shrugged. "Nothing better to do."

Holly finished her call and said, "Bridget can fill in for us."

George paused and smoothed out his beard. "I could drive. We could take our car. I think there's room…"

Mary looked at Holly and Lizzie, and both nodded in agreement.

"Thank you, dear." Mary leaned in to nuzzle George in a hug.

"Oops, I think we have a customer. Back to business for me," Holly whispered, reaching for the cup behind Mary. "Thanks for the wassail!"

"You're very welcome." Mary let go of George. "Do you think Ben would want to go?" she whispered as he started to leave. George needed to return to work, to play his role.

"Not sure. Wouldn't hurt to ask him. Make him feel included. I'll leave it up to you, love."

Two hours later, Mary walked into the cottage to find Ben sipping tea at the table, reading a new book. She sat down to give him all the wonderful details about the baby. Ben and Adam didn't know each other well, but still, she thought Ben might be the teeniest bit glad to hear such wonderful news. When she asked if he wanted to accompany her to see the new bundle of joy, she didn't expect a hearty yes, but the stoic refusal she did receive was equally unexpected. He wasn't so much rude as unemotional, robotic.

Mary thought everyone loved babies and finding out that someone had become a new parent. Wasn't that reason enough to show a sliver of enthusiasm? But Ben didn't appear joyful. He appeared reserved—and distant.

Perhaps he was having one of those episodes again, where he had trouble being social or warm. Despite any progress he made, whatever he was running from always seemed to find him and steal the light from his eyes. She didn't take his mood swings personally anymore. She knew they had nothing to do with her and everything to do with his past. Whatever his mysterious past entailed...

"That's all right," she reassured him. "If you change your mind, let me know."

"I will. Thanks, Mary," he said quietly, flipping the page.

Mary was certain the ride to Bath couldn't be terribly thrilling for George and Fletcher—but if that were true, they weren't showing it. During the entire twenty-five minutes, the girls, all crammed together in the backseat, jabbered away about nothing but babies, babies, babies. They discussed the adorable outfits and rattles and baskets Noelle's baby was about to receive from them, the way babies' skin smelled sweet and felt softer than fleece, and even the cry that only newborns could make. Mary saw Fletcher and George, seated in front, occasionally nod, probably chatting about cars or the weather. They were good sports, and Mary was glad they'd decided to come along and endure all the baby talk.

As they all walked through the sliding doors, Mary noticed the typical hospital odor—that stale mixture of ammonia, broccoli, and sickness. She had to remind herself that hospitals didn't always represent tragedy. They weren't only places where a person went to identify her lifeless son and hold his lifeless hand for the final time; sometimes, they also represented a new beginning. She squeezed George's arm as they entered the lift, and she channeled her anxiety into her grip as they rose higher.

A surprise awaited them outside Noelle's room. Mary saw him first, recognizing the slender frame before he even turned around. Frank O'Neill was the curator of the Chilton Crosse art gallery and a friend of Noelle's.

He swiveled around to see their smiling faces. "Oh, marvelous to see you all!" He gave Holly and Mary a hug with each arm.

"What are you doing here? I didn't expect you!" Holly said. She and Frank had worked together for years, when Holly was his assistant at the gallery.

"Noelle made Adam call me about the baby, so of course, I had to come." He beamed. "Isn't it wonderful?"

"It is," Mary agreed.

Holly lowered her voice to ask Frank as discreetly as possible, "Are you... okay? About Lily?"

Frank's smile faded at the mention of the fiancée who'd recently broken his heart, but Mary could tell he was fighting to stay positive. "I'll be fine," he assured Holly. "She's moved on, and I will, too. Someday."

"You came!" said a voice behind them.

Mary looked around to see Adam emerging from the hospital room, hands raised to greet them.

"Hey, thanks for coming!" If a man could glow, Adam was positively glowing. He would certainly make a wonderful father.

"Want to see my little man?" he asked. "The nurse brought him in a few minutes ago."

"Is it all right with Noelle?" Mary wanted to make sure.

"Absolutely. She's feeling good. In fact, she's been expecting you. Jill, our mate all the way from London, is already in there with her."

He backed away and let them through. George and Fletcher lingered behind with Adam and Frank—a newly formed boys' club.

"Aren't you coming, dear?" Mary asked George.

"No, no," he said. "Wouldn't want to overcrowd the room. You girls go in first. Have your fun." He winked.

Noelle, who was wearing no makeup, seemed as radiant as ever, with her blond hair swept up into a ponytail. At the bed sat a slender, red-haired woman, looking as striking as any model in a magazine, holding out a hand to touch the blue bundled blanket Noelle held.

A chorus of quiet congratulations and compliments came from the girls as they approached the bed. Noelle shifted little Adam ever so slightly, so the new arrivals could see his pink, scrunched-up face. He gurgled and frowned before settling in to sleep again.

"Oh, Noelle, he's completely gorgeous!" Lizzie said, barely containing her squeal.

"He's the cutest thing *ever!*" Holly concurred, cooing at him as she moved closer.

Mary let the girls have the first look and stepped aside to greet Noelle's friend, who had stood to give them room.

"I'm Mary Cartwright."

"Jill Holbrook."

"Oh, I remember you," Mary said. "From Noelle's wedding. You were childhood friends…"

"Yes, that's right." Her perfect green eyes were highlighted with strong dark eye makeup.

"How lovely to know someone from childhood," Mary said. "Aren't those sorts of friendships the rarest treasures?"

"You are so right. I'm thrilled that Noelle and I reconnected. And Adam, as well. We've all been the best of mates ever since. In fact, they're godparents to my little Evie."

"And now, you're godmother to my Adam," Noelle whispered, looking up.

Holly and Lizzie had moved to the same side of the bed, and Mary had a bit of space to stand at the other side. She leaned closer to Noelle, taking in the pudgy, round little face of the newborn wrapped securely in his mother's arms.

"What a blessing," she whispered to Noelle, "to have a son. A precious boy to hold and to love." She tried to control the tremble in her voice, but Noelle had probably caught it.

Noelle squeezed Mary's hand as they locked eyes. The softness in her gaze made Mary wonder if Noelle might suspect how both wonderful and difficult the moment was for her.

When George and Mary arrived at the cottage, Ben was in the process of tying a bin bag. He hadn't expected them back so soon. He had planned on retiring early, before they returned. While they were away, he'd busied himself around the cottage—fixing a leaky tap, replacing dead lightbulbs, and taking out the rubbish. Though George had stopped making lists for him a week ago, Ben consistently found things to do. The chores made him feel better about staying.

"How was your trip?" Ben asked, setting aside the rubbish, and slipped his hands into his jeans pockets. He attempted a warm, interested tone but hoped he wouldn't be given too many details. He wasn't sure he could handle them.

"Wonderful." Mary unwrapped the scarf from her neck.

George helped her out of her coat then removed his own.

"Cute baby," George said, hanging the coats on the nearby rack.

"Oh, he was gorgeous," Mary gushed, using her hands to tell the story. "He opened his eyes for a few seconds—they're dark blue! And he has the tiniest fingernails I've ever seen. I think he's going to be a good baby. He seems calm. Not like some I've seen, even as newborns, fussy and temperamental."

"That's nice," Ben offered, trying to be polite.

"Adam and Noelle will make *such* good parents," she mused. "That's a very lucky little boy."

"Indeed," Ben said. Then he added, "Well, I'm glad you had a nice trip. I'd better turn in—long day tomorrow, up early."

"Goodnight, son," said George.

"Sleep well," Mary added.

"I will. Thanks."

Inside the darkness of Sheldon's room, with only the glow of the moon shining through the narrow window on the opposite side, Ben felt the need to crumble, where it was safe to break down, with no one to watch him and no one to ask questions. But he knew that if he visited that place in his memory, he might never come back. So, standing with his back to the door, he breathed in and fought it. Turning his hands into tight fists at his sides, he clenched his jaw and fought.

He would have to learn to be happy for people who had what he no longer had—and to be glad for people who had new babies and new futures as parents. It wasn't their fault his dreams had ended abruptly and tragically, or that he'd missed his chance to experience everything Mary had just described.

Chapter Fifteen

"Men's courses will foreshadow certain ends, to which, if persevered in, they must lead," said Scrooge. "But if the courses be departed from, the ends will change."

- Charles Dickens

E ARLY THE NEXT MORNING, BEN awoke to Mary's voice, shrieking good news from the next room: "Look! Snow! George, come and see. It's beautiful!"

Instead of rolling out of bed to join them at the window, Ben grunted and flipped onto his side. He covered his ear with a pillow. He respected that other people, like Mary, saw the beauty in snow. They admired the feathery drifts that lilted toward earth from a shapeless sky and the way it blanketed everything—lampposts and cobbled stones and tree branches—and transformed the earth into a bright-white, foreign, temporary land.

But most of Ben's experience with snow had been unfavorable. He rated it anywhere from bothersome, as it wetted trouser legs and needed shoveling away from porches, to dangerous, causing car accidents that clogged hospital emergency rooms and bringing freezing temperatures that left the elderly in homes without heat.

Hours later, his opinion of snow was utterly validated as he lifted a lumber plank high above his head and caught an unexpected drift of snow from the plank smack in his face. He didn't have time—or an extra hand—to wipe it away, so he shook his head with a grumble and carried on.

He and Fletcher, Joe, and Mac had spent the past three hours dismantling all the festival booths. They started early this morning, so that normal village traffic could resume as soon as possible. Ben had thought this meant that the Christmas festivities were well over but remembered that tonight, he had a front-row seat to watch George play Scrooge, and tomorrow night, Mary's ladies' choir would give a Christmas Eve concert to cap off the Dickens Festival.

Ben had just struggled to lug a section of Mrs. Tucker's quilting booth into the van when Mac called his name. Out of breath, Ben pivoted to see him carrying something under his arm. "What's this?"

Mac produced a box with a picture of tools on the outside.

"'Tisn't wrapped. A sort of Christmas present," Mac explained, handing it over. "Thought you could use your own set. Consider this your starter kit."

Ben tilted the box to examine the picture of the kit's contents—nails and screws and hammers and drill bits, even a leveler and portable sander.

"Mac, it's too much. Really…"

Mac chuckled then squinted through the steady snowfall. "Son, you've clocked in nigh a hundred hours for free. This is the least I could do. You're reliable. I can depend on you. And that counts for everything. You've more than earned it."

Ben balanced the gift under one arm and extended his other hand in a hearty shake. "I'll put this to good use."

"I know ye will."

"Hey, you two lazy bums! Back to work!" Fletcher approached them, smiling that generous American smile.

Glad for the distraction, Ben took the opportunity to slip away to the van and stash his early Christmas gift for later. The gesture touched him, and he realized that in the span of a fortnight, he'd grown closer to Mac MacDonald than he ever had his own father.

"Hold still, dear," Mary ordered as she filled in the last corner of George's eyelid with charcoal-gray liner.

"How much longer?" he mumbled.

"There." She stepped back to assess her handiwork. "All finished. That will do, Ebenezer."

George crinkled his thick fake eyebrows and attempted his best stern-scary face, making Mary giggle. "Yes, that will *certainly* do."

"Twenty minutes 'til curtain!" someone called from the other side of the room. The cast and crew of the *Scrooge* production had set up shop inside the church hall. For the past hour, the hall had seen the hustle and bustle of makeup, costumes, and line rehearsing.

Mary could sense George's nerves growing. She gripped his shoulders and looked at him squarely. "You will do *fine*," she said. "More than fine. And if you forget a line, fake it." She leaned in for a whisper. "Or just peek down at your hand." Minutes ago, she'd caught him scribbling lines inside his palm.

"Agreed," Ben said, joining them. "We have full confidence in you. And besides, you had a pair of great coaches."

"I hope I can live up to it."

"Anything I can do?" Ben offered.

"We can't seem to find his hat," Mary said, looking about.

"What does it look like?"

"Gray top hat, black rim."

"No worries. I'll find it," George said, patting Mary's arm. "I think I know where I might've left it. Be right back." He climbed out of his chair to go hat hunting.

A minute later, above the brassy ruckus of overlapping voices finalizing important details, Mary heard a woman screeching, "Help! Please, someone! Help me!"

The volume of the entire room dropped to a hush in a split second as people identified the cry. In the corner, Caroline Lamb, a schoolteacher helping out with the costumes, crouched over her nine-year-old son's limp body. Mary held her breath and watched in horror.

Immediately, a familiar figure rushed toward Caroline. Mary watched Ben, cool and methodical, crouch over James Lamb and ask the mother questions in a calm, low tone as he checked the boy's vital signs. Ben's hands knew exactly what to do.

Mary heard only parts of the frightened mother's broken answers, "Allergy... peanuts... stopped breathing..."

Ben asked, "Do you have epinephrine?"

Caroline shook her head, tears streaming down. "I'd run out... we had an appointment next week, so I thought—"

"Where's the doctor?" Ben shouted at the crowd.

George, who had returned with hat in hand, responded, "He's out of town on holiday."

Mary's chest tightened as Ben asked, "Can you show me his office? Is it nearby?"

Mary and George nodded in sync, and Ben scooped the boy into his arms. A string of curious onlookers followed at a respectful distance as they hurried toward Dr. Andrews's cottage. Fortunately, it was located only a half block from the church. Their hasty footsteps created new imprints in fresh snow. At the door, Mary remembered they had no way inside.

"Mrs. Cox has the key, I think." Mary started to turn and find her.

"There isn't time," Ben said. He handed the limp boy gingerly over to George then slammed his foot against the door. On the third strike, the wood cracked and splintered as the lock gave way.

Ben ushered Caroline inside and relieved George of the boy. Mary and George followed behind, leaving the other villagers outdoors to fret.

Inside, Caroline led the way, past the reception area, through the back door, and into an exam room. Mary flicked on the light switch while Ben placed James on the table.

"Dr. Andrews keeps it here." Caroline pointed to a glass cabinet then rushed back to her son. "It's all right," she whispered, stroking her son's forehead with gentle fingers.

Ben tried the door on the cabinet—it didn't budge. He wriggled out of his jacket and balled it up around his elbow. "Stand back," he said then smashed the glass.

He found what he needed and approached the table.

With steady hands, he held the boy's leg at the kneecap then pushed one end of the injector firmly against the boy's thigh and held it there for several seconds. Mary could see the calm return to Caroline's face, confirming that Ben was doing all the right things.

When he removed the device, he bent over and put his ear against the boy's mouth. "He's breathing."

Caroline gasped her thanks, and Ben stepped back so she could be with her son, whose eyes had fluttered open.

"Mum?" he whispered. She could only sob her response as she rocked him.

Ben ran a hand through his hair, his gaze steady on the boy.

Mary moved toward him, her shoes crunching on broken glass, and said quietly, "That was incredible. You saved his life."

Ben's eyes remained on the boy, but Mary knew he'd heard. He stepped back over to the boy, checking his vital signs again. Caroline gave him the necessary space, and when he nodded his approval, she clasped both hands around one of Ben's. "Thank you."

By then, the whole of the village had been alerted, and Mary could hear voices buzzing in the reception area.

"George, would you go out and tell them it's all right?" she asked. "I think Caroline needs some privacy."

"Certainly." He gave her arm a loving squeeze before he went.

Ben had stepped away from the boy again—this time, clear back to the corner of the opposite wall. Mary couldn't tell if he was shaken from the incident or was simply giving room to mother and child.

She didn't want to pry, but she had to know. Approaching him, she whispered, "How did you know what to do, Ben? You were so calm."

He folded his arms and finally made eye contact. His hesitation told her that he was sifting through his mind for the right words. Finally, he said, "I'm a physician," confirming her suspicion. "A surgeon."

Mary nodded, hoping he would offer more details later.

Within the hour, the little boy was safe and sound in his own cottage, and Mrs. Pickering had cleared away the broken glass while Mac had fixed the busted lock. With all the excitement, some had assumed the play would surely be cancelled, but Mrs. Dalworth announced, "The play must go on." And so it did.

Ironically, the earlier excitement had actually stolen away the nerves of the cast, and they performed flawlessly. George made a brilliant Scrooge, and Mary mouthed half the lines along with him from her seat in the audience, with Ben at her side. After the incident, Ben had insisted on going immediately back to the cottage, likely eager to avoid questions from the villagers. But Mary, knowing how much his support would mean to George, had convinced Ben to stay. She'd suggested that he leave during the curtain call so he could sneak away without being smothered by people's curiosity.

She stole a moment during the Ghost of Christmas Past's speech to glance at Ben—Dr. Ben. He seemed absorbed in the play, and as she saw him in a new light, she realized that the more she discovered about him, the less she actually knew.

"And how about my final line? That got quite a chuckle." George beamed at the thought of it.

"Yes, dear," Mary agreed. "One of the many highlights of the night. You were wonderful." The sleigh bells jingled along with the mare's steps as Mr. Elton steered the carriage around the outskirts of the village.

Mary had thought the sleigh ride would be a nice way to cap off an overly eventful night. She was in desperate need of peace and quiet. So, after the play and a quick round of drinks at the pub to celebrate the play's success, Mary and George had headed for Mr. Elton's horse-drawn carriage at the end of Storey Road.

"I still can't believe what happened," Mary mused, curling the thick blanket closer to her chin. The cold nearly made the ride unbearable. She wasn't certain how long she could last...

"Quite an evening," George agreed.

She attempted to lower her voice so Mr. Elton couldn't hear. "Ben told me something tonight."

"What?"

"Well, I got nosy and asked how he had the knowledge to save that boy's life. And he told me he's a surgeon! Can you believe that?"

George raised his eyebrows. "Well, that explains the way he handled things. I suspected some level of medical knowledge. But a surgeon..."

"Indeed. And it also explains the expensive watch," Mary said.

"And a great many other things. Like how he would never accept money."

"And how he speaks."

"What do you mean?"

"Well, he always sounds educated. Well-refined. Not from around here."

"Excuse me," George protested. "*I'm* from around here."

"Of course, dear." She patted his arm. "You know what I mean. He wasn't exactly the vagabond we first thought he was."

"No, not at all."

"I wonder why he hid it from us all this time," Mary said, more to the night air than to George. "Is he ashamed of it? Of being a surgeon?"

"None of it makes any real sense."

Mary recalled first seeing Ben motionless in the snow, and she watched his shoulders rise and fall with shallow breaths. Weeks later, several pieces of his life's puzzle were still missing. She might not know the details of his past, but Mary was more convinced than ever that a life-altering event had happened to Ben the Surgeon to make him leave his life behind, creep away into a dark night, and end up on her cottage doorstep.

While Mary and George spent the rest of the ride in silence, an awful thought gripped Mary. *What if tonight's events scared Ben off?* She might walk into Mistletoe Cottage to find him gone, for good.

Chapter Sixteen

"I don't know what to do!" cried Scrooge, laughing and crying in the same breath. His own heart laughed: and that was quite enough for him.

~ Charles Dickens

B EN KNEW, AS HE HAD always known, that the moment would come when the memories he'd held at bay for so long would be too strong to ignore. He'd known that one day soon, he would be forced to look them in the eye. All of them.

He left the *Scrooge* performance and, for a moment, gazed at the clear night sky punctuated with stars. He wondered if that moment had drawn near. People in the village were already chattering about him, guessing about his past. And one of his closely held secrets had been discovered. How long before the rest would follow?

Instead of contemplating it further, Ben chose denial. He marched to Mistletoe Cottage in the snow, found a sedative, crawled into bed, and switched off his brain. Everything would have to wait until morning.

When morning came, he still wasn't ready. He blamed the sedative for his grogginess and his inability to focus on the previous night's events. But after a shower and a shave had revived his senses, he knew it was time to move on. He had hoped to stay for at least another week, through the new year, to get his bearings while in the Cotswold bubble. But he'd already let people in too close. He'd let them care. He'd let himself care.

He decided to wait one more day, give Mary her Christmas Day, then leave just as he'd come, under the cover of snow-lit darkness.

As he walked down the hall, he could hear Henry the Robin's song coming from the back garden.

"Happy Christmas Eve," Mary said as Ben entered the sitting room. Mary rocked in her chair, her giant Bible open in her lap.

"Happy Christmas Eve," Ben replied.

He hadn't counted on Mary being up so early. He wasn't prepared for her inevitable barrage of questions. He owed her the truth. But first, he owed it to himself to clear his head.

"I didn't mean to interrupt your reading." He reached for his cap.

"You didn't. I was nearly finished." She closed the book.

"I'm going for a jog."

"It's terribly cold out there," warned Mary.

"I won't be long. Just need to get out for a bit…"

"Certainly," Mary said politely. She opened her Bible again, and he turned the doorknob and disappeared into the frigid air.

Facing certain memories in the light of day was easier than he'd imagined. As Ben jogged, boots crunching in the snow, he scanned the cloudless sky, squinting into the brilliant sunrise. Things did seem brighter, hopeful, in such a beautiful setting.

But actually stepping back into those memories was a darker prospect. Turning behind the church and jogging up that enormous hill, Ben remembered the familiar rush of carrying the boy, hurrying to find the proper medication. Having life and death right there in his hands had been a powerful, frightening, and intoxicating experience—as it had always been for him. Holding a scalpel, fingers poised over a patient, monitors beeping, Ben knew well his purpose. To repair. To heal. To nudge a patient from the edge of death, back toward life.

Even with all his education behind him, even after performing hundreds of surgeries, he still carried the weight of that responsibility. He never took his role for granted or let go of the panic deep inside his gut, telling him that he alone could be the reason someone didn't make it off that table. And never had he felt that responsibility more than he had on his final day as a surgeon.

On that morning, he had prepped for a routine bypass, feeling edgier than usual. He'd been having nightmares again. Six months had passed since the funeral. He had pressed on, insisting on working full hours, even overtime. He'd ignored the advice of his supervisor, who'd suggested a leave of absence to get grief counseling. That would have been the worst possible thing for Ben. Work was what he *needed*—the only thing he needed.

The nightmares, always the same, magically disappeared sometime during those months, and he thought he was done with them. But the few nights before that particular surgery, they'd haunted him again. His wife, Amanda, stood holding their child just out of his reach, crying for his help. He would run to them but always smack up against a glass wall standing between them. He tried again and again, until his shoulder throbbed with pain, even through the dream. He always yelled back, reassuring Amanda that he would save them. Amanda nodded, clutching their baby daughter. Then Amanda would walk backward, her face gaunt and stoic, until the darkness swallowed them both whole. Often at that point, Ben woke up screaming her name.

The nightmare, more vivid than ever, had occurred again the night before what would become his final surgery. And he couldn't shake it. Ben stood in the operating theater before the cardiac patient, surrounded by nurses and techs. Above, in the gallery, a new batch of residents watched him perform the routine surgery, which Ben had performed so many times that he'd lost count. But as his scalpel touched the patient, he sensed an unaccountable panic bubbling up. His vision began to blur, and his thoughts became murky. Even his hearing seemed watery as he strained to hear the nurse beside him.

"Dr. Granger?" Her voice sounded hollow and faraway, though she was standing right next to him.

A panic attack, he thought. *Right here, in the middle of a surgery.* His worst professional nightmare.

He fought against it, but the panic took over. His heart raced, and his head tingled. After an eternity, his senses snapped back quite suddenly. His vision cleared, and his hearing returned. He felt shaken but centered.

"Dr. Granger?" the nurse said again, touching his shoulder.

"I'm fine," he assured everyone. "Fine." To them, he'd hopefully looked like a man only taking a strong pause. Surely they hadn't sensed the panic that had churned inside. He could recover.

Taking a breath, Ben began the procedure. He somehow found his bearings; his confidence came back. But midway through, something went terribly wrong. The panic rushed in again, and his finger slipped, slicing his blade through a ventricle.

Ben struggled to maintain his focus, despite the frantic beeping of monitors, the scrambling of the anesthesiologist, and the nurses' gasps. Miraculously, Ben was able to push through the chaos, high on adrenaline, to repair the damage in time to fix what he'd broken.

But afterward, hunched over and trembling in a dark corner of his office, he was convinced his career was over. After hearing about the incident, his supervisor ordered a mandatory leave of absence but reassured Ben that he would have his place back when he returned. The incident in the operating room wasn't an unforgivable sin.

But Ben had already given up on himself. He'd made the decision in that dark corner. He couldn't do it anymore—keep up appearances, pretending he was fine. It was all over. And part of him felt nothing but relief.

He scribbled his resignation on a sticky note and slapped it on his supervisor's door. Then he rushed to his flat, texted his good friend Martin a vague explanation about life changes and the need to escape, packed a bag, and left his mobile phone behind. He took a taxi to the edge of London and began to walk. He wandered for weeks, sleeping in empty barns or renting a room at a random pub. He even slept on a grassy patch under a tree in the countryside. He didn't care. His comfort didn't matter. Nothing mattered anymore.

Finally, in an unfamiliar Cotswold village, he'd collapsed in the middle of a street, near someone's doorstep. That someone had taken him in and opened her home. She'd given him respite and so much more...

Reaching the top of the hill, Ben stopped and bent over, resting his hands on his knees as his breath puffed out in vapors. The stinging inside his lungs was almost unbearable, but at least he felt something.

After a moment, he stretched to his full height, raising his hands high above his head, and looked at the sky. A purple-and-orange sunrise lay before him, more beautiful than any he'd ever seen. He wished Amanda could have been there with him.

Hours later, Ben fought off a wave of guilt as he walked with George up to the church for the final night of activities. He owed George and Mary at least a warning that he would be leaving a bit sooner than they'd probably expected. *But why ruin their Christmas Eve?*

Near the church, the nativity spotlight beamed on Holly, who was wearing a powder-blue dress and head covering. Ben wondered if she was cold. He squinted and noticed a little commotion on Joseph's— or Fletcher's—part. He had abandoned his staff and was facing Holly squarely. They were supposed to be as still as statues, but Fletcher had reached inside his costume and was digging something out. George had seen it, too. He and Ben paused in the street.

"Let's go see," George suggested, taking a detour toward the nativity, and Ben followed.

Though he stood well behind the growing circle of onlookers, Ben was taller than nearly everyone else in the crowd, so he had a clear line of vision. George had to peer in between a couple of tourists to see.

Something was happening, something orchestrated. Ben watched Holly's face shift from confusion to growing surprise—one arm holding the baby Jesus, a doll, while her other hand reached up to clamp her mouth shut. Her eyes grew wide, staring at the open ring box in Fletcher's hand. He was trembling, down on one knee, and he mumbled something to her through his fake beard. Holly paused and nodded, hand still clamped over her mouth. Fletcher smiled and swooped her up in a strong embrace as the crowd cheered.

The proposal hadn't surprised Ben—he'd overheard Fletcher the other day as they were clearing away the booths, asking Adam how he'd proposed to Noelle. *Odd, though, that he would choose a nativity scene for a proposal.* But, as Ben thought about it, the proposal also seemed unique—and rather appropriate. *Weren't Mary and Joseph engaged when she gave birth to Jesus?* And what better way to surprise Holly than to pop the question on Christmas Eve? A night to remember.

"Good for them," George said then resumed his walk as Ben trailed behind.

They had arrived early for the concert, to see if the choir needed a hand in moving anything on or off the stage. The ladies began their warm-up, with only twenty minutes until the concert. After helping move a couple of chairs offstage, Ben and George took their seats up front, where they each studied a paper program Mary had thrust into their hands when they first arrived.

"Mr. Granger? I mean... Dr. Granger?" Ben heard from behind. He looked around to see Caroline Lamb shyly entering his pew with her little boy.

"Hi," Ben said, hoping to put him at ease.

"Dear, tell him what we said," Caroline coached her son in a whisper.

"Thank you," the boy told Ben, "for saving me."

"You're quite welcome. I'm glad you're all right."

Caroline opened her mouth to speak, her bottom lip trembling. "Thank you so much for yesterday. I don't know how I can ever—"

"It's okay," Ben said. "It all worked out."

"I should have had the medicine with me," she explained. "I always carry it in my bag, but I didn't have a spare this time. I felt like such a fool. And if you hadn't been there to get into Dr. Andrews's office for us, I can't imagine..."

Ben reached out to pat her hand as a tear splashed down her cheek. "It wasn't your fault. You can't blame yourself." Hearing those words come out of his own mouth, Ben wondered if he really meant them. He didn't believe them in his own case, so why should he utter them so assuredly to someone else?

"You'll never know how grateful I am." She slipped back out of the pew with the boy as quietly as she'd entered.

"Ben!" Mary approached him, her face frantic.

"What's wrong?"

"Mrs. O'Grady. She's taken ill. She's just phoned and said she won't make it here after all."

"I'm sorry?" He didn't understand what the woman's absence could possibly have had to do with him.

"She's our *pianist*," Mary said, emphasizing the word so he would understand.

"Oh." The light came on. "No. No, no, no..." Ben shook his head and raised his hands.

"But you'd be brilliant!" she pleaded. "No trouble at all for you. And it's only three songs, not even the whole concert. The rest is a capella."

"Mary, I'm sorry. I just can't—"

"Ben, please. I'm begging you. The ladies need you." She paused. "*I need you.*"

He saw the desperation in her eyes. She was making a refusal absolutely impossible.

He blew out a long sigh. "Right, then. I'll do it."

"Bless you!" She reached over and clasped his cheeks with her cold hands, giving his forehead a quick peck.

She jounced back to her place in the choir, and Ben asked George with a wince, "What have I just done?"

"What I do every single day—anything Mary says." He grinned, slapping Ben on the back as he got up to do his duty.

Mary was right—the songs themselves were no trouble for him. Ben glanced at the simple sheet music before rehearsing them once through with the choir, which more than adequately prepared him for the concert. Sight-reading had never been a problem for him.

But as he watched people file in, mulling about to find seats, his nerves gathered strength. He'd played concerts as a teenager, with all eyes on him, but that had been decades ago.

Soon, the vicar's wife approached center stage, holding her baton and welcoming the crowd, whose conversations had dwindled to a few whispers. Ben's fingers hovered over the keys, ready for her baton's command. He played shyly at first, perhaps too shyly, being careful not to overpower the ladies' voices as they sang "O Holy Night." He'd never accompanied voices before. Following her baton accurately was a bit of a challenge, as he could barely see it from where he was sitting. But he got through it and waited his turn through four a capella songs, until they reached "Ding Dong Merrily on High." Then he waited a little more before the grand finale, "Angels We Have Heard on High." The crowd appeared to enjoy it, clapping and cheering after the final song. Ben regretted ever turning Mary down in the first place—what had it really cost him to help her out?

When the clapping subsided, the vicar's wife started to thank the audience, but Mary interrupted to whisper something to her.

"Oh, yes—and we want to thank Dr. Ben Granger, nephew to Mary Cartwright, for stepping in at the last minute. Wasn't he wonderful?"

More applause followed. Embarrassed, Ben dipped his head in acknowledgment then exited the piano's nook.

"Oh, Ben, that was marvelous." Mary approached him as the crowd dispersed, and she leaned in to give him a hug. "You're a lifesaver!" She caught her own play on words and said sheepishly, "Both figuratively and literally, I suppose…"

"No trouble at all. Glad to help out."

A few of Mary's friends stood behind her, taking turns to compliment his playing.

"Hey, nice job, Doc!" Ben turned around to see Adam grinning. "Where'd you learn to play like that?"

Ben shrugged. "Music lessons as a boy. Drudgery."

"Well, look who I brought with me." Adam stepped aside to reveal his wife, Noelle, holding their brand-new baby boy. Ben could only see the center of his pink face, eyes closed in tiny slits. The rest of him was wrapped up tight in a fleecy blue blanket.

"Meet my namesake. Adam Junior." Adam pulled back the edge of the blanket so Ben could get a better look.

Ben knew what he was supposed to say. *Congratulations, beautiful baby, how much did he weigh?* But none of it came through. All he could do was stare at the button nose and remember another button nose: a baby almost that same size, lifeless, whom he'd held for ten minutes then given up to a nurse, his arms trembling and mind reeling.

"I'm… happy for you," Ben managed to utter then stepped back to find the air. The church felt stifling and suffocating. People had begun exiting through the back, and Mary grabbed Ben's arm. "We're all going down to the pub. Christmas Eve celebration! Drinks are on Joe."

Ben nodded to let her know he understood. "You go on." He slipped through a side entrance close by, tipping the door shut behind him. He hadn't even known where it led, only that it led away from that baby, away from that reminder.

He remained in the narrow hallway, his back flush against the cold stone wall, and made himself breathe. *In. Out. In. Out.* His breaths came in gasps. He traced the angled shadow on the opposite wall with his eyes, trying to steady his focus on something. He followed the sharp line up to the corner then down again to the opposite corner, until his breathing slowed.

Several minutes passed before he was sure he wouldn't black out, and by the time he reached out to turn the brass knob, he felt marginally better, at least physically.

The church was completely empty, and Ben realized that the thought of singing Christmas carols in a cheery pub nearly made him nauseated. They would make a mockery of the anguish going on inside him. Christmas made less sense than ever, though he'd been a crucial part of the celebration just an hour earlier, and even in the weeks before, he'd constructed a manger for the baby Jesus. *What have I been doing all this time? Playing a role?*

His legs carried him over to a center pew up front. Unable to go any farther, he slumped down, dead weight. All of him felt dead.

"You go on, dear. I've left something behind. I'll return in a few minutes," Mary promised George at the pub's door.

"Are you sure?"

"I'm sure." She patted his arm and headed off for the church.

She had seen the way Ben looked at that baby. He'd tried to cover the shift in his gaze, but he hadn't fooled her.

After a chilling walk, she opened the church door with a grunt and saw him immediately, hunched over in a pew. Obviously a broken man. Mary only hoped he wasn't broken beyond repair.

She walked quietly, shrugging off her nerves. *Am I intruding? What if I say the wrong thing?* Still, she followed her intuition and pressed on. Halfway down the aisle, she saw Ben turn with a start.

"I'm sorry," she said. "I didn't mean to interrupt."

He turned back around and folded his hands over the pew in front of him. She recognized a flash of silver between his fingers—the angel she'd found beside him in the snow.

She assumed the last thing he wanted was company, but she'd danced around the question for far too long. It was time. It was Christmas Eve, he was in pain, and it was time. No more messing about.

She sat down beside him, leaving a bit of space between them. After a moment, Mary spoke. "Tell me, Ben."

He inhaled a deep, conscious breath, and she wondered if he'd been crying before she came in. He cleared his throat and folded his fingers together—the angel disappeared between his palms.

Ben stared up at the stained glass as he spoke. "Her name was Amanda. We were married thirteen years ago. University sweethearts. We were one of those couples you envy and even sort of hate for being so completely in love. We were best friends. She knew everything about me—every weakness, every insecurity. And she never held them against me." He reached up to wipe his nose then refolded his hands. "She helped me work my way through med school without a single complaint. Then she endured my residency and new position on staff. The long hours, the nights on call, the boring parties. All of it."

Mary stared ahead as he spoke. Picturing her, Mary wondered how pretty Amanda was, what color her hair might've been, and how she and Ben had looked together.

"The time came to start a family, and we thought it would be easy, like everything else that came to us. But after the first year, we realized it wouldn't be... easy. So, we went through the necessary tests and treatments and trials. We did it for two years, barely hanging on. And after three miscarriages, she got pregnant again."

Mary felt her throat catch with excitement, then she remembered his brokenness. His story wouldn't end well.

Ben's voice remained even and low—detached. "It was a Tuesday night, a busy one for me. Amanda was in her eighth month but was having some difficulties. Eclampsia—high blood pressure," he clarified. "It can be dangerous, so she was on bed rest. Her mother was able to come and help during days, and I got the night shift."

He peered into his hands and rubbed the angel with his thumb. "Anyway, that night, I was offered a case—a surgery I'd never done before, one I'd been hoping for, talking about for months. I'd already worked a thirteen-hour shift and was knackered. But Amanda insisted over the phone. It was a chance I couldn't miss, she said. She and the baby would be fine. She was about to go to sleep anyway and would see me in the morning. So, I took the case. And when I got home..."

Mary heard his breath change. She wanted to help somehow, offer comfort, but she had to stay out of the way.

"I found her on the floor, beside the bed, unconscious but still breathing. She must've fainted trying to get out of bed and hit her head. The eclampsia was likely a factor, but the doctors were never sure. I rushed to her side, cradled her with one hand and rang for an ambulance with the other. I talked to her, stroked her hair for the eternity it took the ambulance to arrive, praying she would just open her eyes. A flutter, anything." He was talking to the air as if seeing the scene all over again. "Please, God. Just a sign. But it didn't come. We rode in the ambulance, and they delivered the baby an hour later at the hospital. Stillborn. Angelina was her name. I held her, memorized her features. The most beautiful hair... honey-colored. Like Amanda's. And then they took her away from me. Amanda was still critical—she'd had a brain hemorrhage. I stayed with her that night, held her hand, told her about Angelina. Begged her to fight, to stay with me. I couldn't lose them both. But she died four and a half hours later. She took her last breath at 5:22 a.m."

For the first time, he made eye contact with Mary, his gaze watery and helpless, like a little boy's. But there was anger, too, as he squinted through the tears, causing one to slide down his cheek. "This was my fault. I was daft and selfish, choosing a prestigious case over my own wife. I should have been there with her—I could have saved her, called sooner for help. And my baby girl..."

His face twisted into a sob, and Mary leaned in to catch him as he dipped toward her, burying his face in her shoulder. He gripped her tightly, weeping into the soft cotton fabric of her coat. The sound echoed inside the church's walls.

"It's okay," she whispered. "You're all right." She patted his back and waited for him to finish, fighting back her own tears. She could break down later, privately. She had to be the strong one now.

Soon, the sobs turned to slower breaths, and Ben backed away, wiping his eyes with his fingers. "I'm so sorry..." he whispered.

"For what?"

"Losing control."

"Ben." She waited until he made eye contact. "You *needed* to lose control. It was high time."

He cast his eyes downward.

"You've been through a horrific trauma," she whispered, praying for all the right words. "You lived through hell, and only a short time ago. And I'd venture that you haven't told this story to another soul since it happened."

He nodded.

"I'm honored that you told me. I'm honored to know about your wife, your daughter. They deserve to be talked about. Remembered."

Ben flicked away another tear. "Thank you."

"And I have news for you."

"What?"

"It wasn't your fault. You were a loving husband, a loving father-to-be. These deaths—these losses—are not on your head. You are *not* to blame."

Ben's tone became frustrated, even angry. "I'm a rational man, Mary. I know better than that. If I'd rejected the case and gone home instead, I would have saved her. At least gotten her help in time. She would be with me, right here, today. But instead, I saved a stranger's life and lost my family."

"*How* do you know?" Mary urged. "How do you know, one hundred percent, that she wouldn't have died, anyway? Yes, you're a rational man. So, can you guarantee that your presence would've prevented that? Absolutely guaranteed?"

He paused then relented. "No. But it might have. You don't understand. I was a workaholic. My career was everything. More important than my family."

"Rubbish!" Mary said more firmly than she meant. "You're telling yourself that so you can continue feeling guilty. You loved your wife—I can see it in your eyes, hear it in your voice. Look at the angel you cling to—the one you had in your hand the night you collapsed. You loved them both more than any surgery, more than any job. That night was a horrible tragedy. But it wasn't your fault."

For a second, she thought he might've believed her, but then he retorted with, "Well, if it wasn't my fault, then maybe it was God's. He's in control of everything, isn't He? Why would He allow it? Amanda didn't do anything wrong. She was blameless. So was my little girl. Why couldn't He have taken me instead?" His eyes filled with anguish again.

"Oh, Ben." Mary shook her head. "Why does it have to be *anyone's* fault? Does that make it easier to accept? Does that bring them back to you?"

Ben shook his head. "No. It doesn't."

She calmed her voice, knowing where she had to go next but not knowing if she had the strength to do it. "Look. I, of all people, understand wanting to blame someone and needing to ask, 'What if?' Don't you think I asked myself that question a million times after Sheldon's death? *What if I had insisted he not go to London? What if that car had made its left turn five seconds later?* But I've learned that it changes nothing. What-ifs are poison. Those questions are futile. They didn't bring Sheldon back to me. And I discovered something. I was damaging his memory by obsessing about it. I was wasting time focusing on the questions rather than on the precious time he'd spent with me on this earth. There comes a time for acceptance. For faith. For letting go, just a little bit. Not of your memories or of your daughter and wife—but of the blame. Of the guilt. Ben, that sort of guilt will destroy you. It nearly destroyed me."

Somewhere in the middle of her speech, Ben had softened. She couldn't find the anger in his eyes anymore. In fact, the intensity of his expression told her he had soaked in every word.

He opened his mouth as if he were about to speak, but nothing came out. He tried again in a whisper, "How? How do I get there? To your place of acceptance? I don't think I can..."

"It will come," she said, placing a hand on top of his. "It takes time. You must give yourself time. There's no other way."

Her hand left his, to reach for the Bible in the pew. She put on her glasses as she spoke. "I know you might not want to hear this, but there's a verse that absolutely got me through those early days. And although it didn't fully answer the question of why, it gave me inexplicable comfort."

She flipped through until she found the right passage in Psalms 139. She knew it by heart but didn't trust her weary mind to be accurate. She read aloud: "'For You created my inmost being; You knit me together in my mother's womb... All the days ordained for me were written in

Your book before one of them came to be.'" She removed her glasses to look at Ben again. "That tells me that every person, every creature who is born, has a very specific number of days to live on this earth. 'Ordained,' it says. Don't you see? We *have* no power over those ordained days. They're set in stone. Permanent. There is nothing I could've done to help Sheldon. It was his time to go, no matter if I wasn't ready for it. His days were already ordained for him. Just like Amanda's. And your little girl's." She said her next words slowly, purposefully: "There is *nothing* that you could have done to change that. It was entirely out of your hands."

Sharing scripture was a great risk—it might even do the opposite of what she hoped for. He might shut down or close off as he mentally scoffed at her ridiculous theories. But after a moment, she saw in his eyes a difference: an acknowledgment that what she had said might— just *might*—hold a little merit.

"Thank you," he whispered, reaching for a hug. This time, it wasn't a desperate, mournful hug but a solid one—a little less broken.

He leaned away, rubbing his face and sighing deeply. "I've kept you from your party."

"No, you haven't. I would've rather been here than anywhere else."

Ben reached down and squeezed her hand, and she could tell her time was up. He needed to sort through things on his own.

She replaced the Bible and stood, feeling somehow that her talk had helped her even more than it might've helped Ben. She felt oddly renewed, and the image of Sheldon appeared fresh in her mind. She realized tears had formed, knowing that her Sheldon might have helped someone else find his way tonight...

After Mary left, Ben opened the Bible again, found the passage she'd read to him, and kept on reading. Mary's words resonated in his mind as he thumbed through page after page. He could hear her intent and, beneath it, an earnest and steadfast faith. She had spoken from heartbreaking experience, and she had given Ben precisely what he'd needed. The truth. He had longed to hear it for months, and finally, someone found the courage to offer it.

He ached for Mary's kind of faith, one that could anchor him. He always had. He'd tried to fill that void all his life with good grades and accomplishments, with a career, and even with a marriage and fatherhood. But everything was fallible. Even a wife, or a child, could be taken away in a single heartbeat. And so, when everything else was gone, what else was left?

Mary's advice hadn't made him ache any less for Amanda or Angelina. It hadn't resolved all his questions or even diminished all the anger and guilt he still held. But in the two hours since their conversation, Ben had started to challenge the thought patterns and beliefs he'd so stubbornly clung to for months. He analyzed his life from a different angle, inside a new dimension. His first instinct had been to fight any change in thought, but what Mary had spoken was too powerful. It made too much sense to him. He had experienced nothing less than an epiphany.

Ben rose from the pew as if he were an old man. His bones creaked, and his muscles quivered. Yet, inside, he felt... relaxed. People always spoke of a calm before the storm. But what about the calm after a storm? After tears have been shed, demons have been confronted, battled, and slayed, and fallacies have been brought to light? He'd experienced a near euphoria, much like a cool-down after a long, exhausting workout, after the body has been tested to its limits, endured hardship and discomfort, then come out the other side. A relaxed, easy, exhilarating calm sets in.

Ben made his way out of the church doors, in no hurry, knowing he'd experienced a clear change of heart, similar to what Scrooge experienced on his own Christmas Eve. There was no other way to describe it. Hope had sprung where only despair had been. Excitement grew where dullness had festered. He wasn't sure how a newfound hope would influence his future days. But he was actually able to *picture* future days with more than just dread or uncertainty. The world contained color again. There was life still to be lived—and people still to love, as the villagers in Chilton Crosse had shown him. They had no reason to love him or care about him. But still, they had.

Ben walked out into the falling snow and paused. He could see the entire village from the spot where he stood—the shops, the pub, and Mistletoe Cottage at the end of the street, its lights twinkling in the darkness. Not a soul was in sight so late on Christmas Eve.

He started to walk. Everywhere. On empty pavements in front of the shops. On the fringes of the village behind Storey Road. On vacant country roads. The cold didn't affect him—he was used to it, numb to it. Each step brought him closer to sorting out his epiphany, filling in the gaps and answering the questions. He turned them over and over in his mind until he was sure of something. And when he was sure, he went to the only place that made sense to him in that moment.

Dark and empty, the nativity was lit only by the full moon. Ben approached the rugged manger he'd crafted with his own hands. He saw the baby inside: a doll wrapped lovingly in a blanket. Jesus.

Before that night, before knowing Mary Cartwright and her faith in this child, Ben hadn't thought much of Jesus beyond a few Bible stories. But *this* was the source of her faith—this person, this God. He was the reason she was able to live life with such peace and joy, even in the face of unspeakable tragedy. *What is it about Him that gives people such hope?*

Ben wanted to know more. He had to know more. And so…

No one in the village saw the dark shadow kneel, stamping deep craters in the powdery snow. No one heard the thump of his hopeful heart or saw the tremble in his fingers as he clutched the silver angel. And no one could hear the earnest, searching prayer he uttered to a small baby lying in a manger.

Other Books by Traci Borum

Painting the Moon (Chilton Crosse #1)
Finding the Rainbow (Chilton Crosse #2)

Acknowledgements

To my family—especially my mother, Pat, and my sister, Karen. Your support means everything, and your encouragement keeps me strong and motivated.

To my father, who read this book several months before he passed away. I'm honored he read it, and I'm so grateful for his encouragement in my writing, and more especially, in my life.

To my dearest friends and to those who continue to be supportive of my writer's journey: Augusta Malvagno, Sandy Graham, Becky Bray, Karen Peterson, Doris Lininger, the TJC family, the Red Adept authors, and my beloved Commandos.

To Linda Bratcher, for using her eagle eye on this manuscript. Your help and friendship is so appreciated!

To Rich Sawrey and Kate Manning, who guided me through the British-isms. Thanks for taking the time out of your busy schedules to read the book! Also thanks to Jaimee Sawrey and DeeAnna Manning for putting me in contact with Rich and Kate.

To Dr. David Dykes, whose encouragement is so appreciated. And it was one of his amazing sermons that triggered the inspiration for the spiritual through line of this novel. I remember scrawling notes on the worship program so I wouldn't forget them!

To Sue Willis and Tami Tidwell, whose excitement always makes me smile. Y'all are the best!

Special thanks to my publisher, Lynn McNamee, whose professionalism, knowledge, and ambition have helped to create an amazing publishing company that produces high-quality books. I'm honored to be on board with Red Adept. Also special thanks to my editor,

Stefanie Spangler Buswell, whose attention to detail is remarkable. She allowed this book to be what it was meant to be.

To the entire Red Adept team, especially Jessica Anderegg and Kris James, as well as Streetlight Graphics, particularly Glendon Haddix. This novel is what it is because of your diligence, dedication, and talents. I'm so grateful to you.

To Renina Baker at Motophoto for my author photo.

Finally, all thanks to Jesus, who makes everything in this life worthwhile. He is the Source.

About the Author

TRACI BORUM IS A WRITING teacher and native Texan. She's also an avid reader of women's fiction, most especially Elin Hilderbrand and Rosamunde Pilcher novels. Since the age of 12, she's written poetry, short stories, magazine articles, and novels.

Traci also adores all things British. She even owns a British dog (Corgi) and is completely addicted to Masterpiece Theater—must be all those dreamy accents! Aside from having big dreams of getting a book published, it's the little things that make her the happiest: deep talks with friends, a strong cup of hot chocolate, a hearty game of fetch with her Corgi, and puffy white Texas clouds always reminding her to "look up, slow down, enjoy your life."

Made in the USA
Charleston, SC
02 August 2015